The Crone's Tales

The Crone's Tales

Fables for New Times

J. D. Jahn

atmosphere press

For Avery and Jude, now and future readers.

And, as ever, for Elizabeth.

To the Mysterious Old Woman

I hope this is what you expected of me when you left these stories on the F Train that night months ago. If so, perhaps, you will now leave me alone.

There I was, minding my own business on a nearly empty car, along with some of the subway regulars: raucous youths in hoodies and flashy Nikes, earbuds in and voices loud; a day laborer, dazed by exhaustion, heading for Ditmars or Kings Highway; the Latina mother and her wide-eyed child; an elderly man reading a smudged Chinese newspaper; the teenager with her nose buried in her device; and so on...almost all of us (except the youths) dutifully wearing masks and keeping our social distance, as expected.

I took you for another of New York's countless homeless, mumbling to yourself and huddled in your filthy blankets, your support dog dozing at your feet and your cat glaring from your lap—someone better to avoid than to engage.

Just as we pulled into the Fourth and Smith Street stop, you withdrew a package of stained brown paper wrapped in twine from the folds of your dusky cloak and laid it pointedly on priority seating beside you. Then, you looked me full in the eye and nodded, just once.

The MTA's admonishment, *See Something, Say Something*, flashed through my mind, but the deliberate nature of your action and your abrupt exit when the doors slid open left me curiously paralyzed—and a little reckless. What in that package could be so important, and what did you plan for it...or for me?

When later I read the quaint stories you'd left, they seemed so remote and yet so immediate, too. In one quirky tale after the other, I thought I saw glimmerings of your purpose, and I wondered if, somehow, you intended them specifically for me.

From time to time ever since, I'd glimpse you, your dog and cat hovering just at the edge of my vision or vanishing around a corner or, sometimes, even in my dreams—a shadowy figure with a cane, waiting and watching...but for what?

So, I offer those tales just as I found them: in your old style and odd vocabulary. I can only hope that I've correctly guessed your intentions.

If not, you obviously know how to find me.

These Be My Tales—

Tale the First
A Prince of the Forest

Once upon a time when Brilliant Ben was born, Lady Portentia appeared in her robes of sable to warn his proud parents that their prince's feet must ne'er touch the earth.

"Why ever not?" asked Brilliant Ben's father, Kindly King Charles.

"Yes, why not indeed?" echoed Brilliant Ben's mother, Goodly Queen Millicent.

"Your son is special," warned Lady Portentia ominously. "He is not like others. He is a prince who must be carried about in a golden chair. Ye shall thank me for this advice one day," said she; and then she vanished to God-knows-where.

Vigilant were Kindly King Charles and Goodly Queen Millicent e'er to heed Lady Portentia's portent. When Brilliant Ben was but an infant, two nurses stood watch o'er his crib by night and day, to be certain that he tumbled not out onto the ground.

When Brilliant Ben grew into a lad, two guards did stand their watch, both by night and day, to see that his feet ne'er touched ground. They carried him to chapel and set him down there in his royal pew. They carried him home once more and placed him at the dinner table, where Goodly Queen Millicent and Kindly King Charles asked him how the sermon had been. These two guards—named Cliffton and Erik, by-the-by—carried Brilliant Ben to his royal bed at night and stood near as Good Queen Millicent and Kindly King Charles tucked him in, told him a tale, and kissed him goodnight.

In this manner did Brilliant Ben grow into a young man; nor did he ever set foot upon dirt or grass or stone. When he went abroad into the country, Cliffton and Erik carried him through towns and villages in a golden chair, Erik in the front and Cliffton in the rear.

All the good people in the realm cheered their fair prince as he was carted by.

"There goes Prince Brilliant Ben," so cheered they all. "His feet must ne'er touch the ground. Isn't he brilliant?" And all did cheer the more.

Nor was Brilliant Ben called "brilliant" for nothing. Anon, he began to note that other young men were not carried about in golden chairs. In sooth, at that time of our world most young men walked where'er they wished to go.

And in walking, these young men did have adventures brave and meet young ladies fair, who also were walking where'er they desired. The young men played games that required them to run up and down; they explored forests and streams and helped their agèd parents by carrying food and drink home from the market.

"Why on earth can I not do the same?" reasoned the brilliant youth unto himself. "See the happiness on the young men's faces! See how their parents love them for the help and support they provide! Look at the lovely young maids they meet along their way!

"Whysoe'er shouldst I not enjoy the same? And wherefore am I bound unto this gilded chair? Am I not a prince o' the realm and mine own self after all?" he concluded.

So it was that one day, as Brilliant Ben was thinking these same thoughts and more like them, he observed how grey Erik's hair had become. He noted how Cliffton no longer stood tall and proud behind his chair but had instead become bent. He regarded how slowly his two loyal guards moved along the roadway as they carried him and his golden chair; and he heard how they groaned (e'er so softly, to be sure) when they stooped to pick up the golden chair with him within.

"In truth, 'tis a rather elaborate chair, with a good many decorations on it," Brilliant Ben reflected.

That very afternoon, the three of them entered a deep forest. Therein, Brilliant Ben did call aloud to Cliffton and to Erik: "Dear friends, let us take our rest, for 'tis wondrously cool here in the shade of these tall trees and I, for one, would fain ha' me a nap."

Sans argument or objection of any kind, Erik and Cliffton lowered the great golden chair onto the grass, and then lowered they themselves to the ground as well. In no time, was this leafy glen filled with echoes of their prodigious snoring.

Then, Prince Brilliant Ben did turn himself sideways, e'er so slowly, in his golden chair. He stretched out his princely legs over its rail and, with the greatest care, placed his slippered feet on the ground—first the right foot, then the left.

Tall stood Prince Brilliant Ben upon the soft grass of the forest. It was cool and damp through his slippers of blue velvet. Then, Brilliant Ben desired to feel the earth beneath his feet, so he bent down and slipped off his velvet slippers—first the right slipper, and then the left. He 'gan to pace into the forest.

How cool the earth felt and how the grass caressed the soles of his feet! Oh, how very much the prince wished the feeling would last forever, for it was a true wonder he had ne'er felt before!

"At last," murmured he unto himself. "This is where I belong. This joy, this grass, this dappled light and all: 'tis what I was born for."

As Ben trod deeper into the forest, he noted his legs growing stiff and heavy. "Ah, how woefully out of shape I am," mused he.

Then the prince noted how his feet were sinking all the deeper into the soft, cool earth, so deep, in sooth, that they disappeared beneath the grass. Deeper and deeper did his feet sink, down into the cool, soft earth—so deep that Brilliant Ben suddenly felt the hidden, dark water that flows, hidden in silence, 'neath the forest floor.

As his feet touched this dark water, the prince's legs stopped moving. Then turned they into a slender trunk of greenwood that rose up to the sky. There and then spread wide the prince's arms, and from the fingers of his royal hands grew a hundred and three bright, green leaves. Prince Brilliant Ben felt the sun warm his head, which now was also green and leafy. He felt the summer's breeze busy among his many branches.

Far below, Prince Brilliant Ben spied Erik and Cliffton wake from their dreary naps, look 'round and utter cries of terror and dismay. "Prince Brilliant, Prince Brilliant," they cried, but the prince did not answer, for there was a nest of newly hatched sparrows perched near to his wooden lips and he durst not disturb them.

Anon was the whole, dark forest filled with the king's men, a-calling the prince's name and saying, "Woe unto us; we have lost Prince Brilliant Ben."

"I'm right here," Brilliant Ben murmured; but he heard another voice whisper: "They can't hear thee, thou knowst. I'm not e'en sure they know how to listen."

Brilliant Ben was amazed. "And who might thou be?" he rustled.

"I am thy brother, Prince Fantastic Frank," the tree whispered. "Wouldst thou mind moving thy limb but a bit? You're blocking my sunlight."

"But, what are we doing here?" asked Prince Brilliant Ben. And his voice in his own ears did sound like the rustling the wind makes as it stirs the tree branches and leaves.

"We are living our lives, providing shade and clearing the air," answered Fantastic Frank. "What more should princes of this earth be doing?"

Brilliant Ben looked down at his long, straight trunk. He looked at his arms, long and abustle with bright, green leaves. The brush of the baby sparrows' bristle feathers against his cheek as they jostled and bumped one another, vying for their mother's attention, thrilled him to his very roots.

"Does this happen oft?" asked Prince Brilliant Ben.

"All the time," replied Fantastic Frank. And the other trees chimed in, in their whispery voices: "It happens all the time," said they.

Far below, the prince watched his parents, Kindly King Charles and Goodly Queen Millicent, sadly walking. The Lady Portentia, in her dark robes, paced right behind them. "What did I tell ye?" she cried. "What warned ye I? We'll be out of princes ere long, if ye two take not more care!"

"I rather wish, dear sister, that you would go back to God-knows-where," muttered Goodly Queen Millicent, though she immediately regretted her remark.

"I am afraid 'tis but a sad fact of our times," reflected Kindly King Charles morosely. "Our daughters and our sons must find their own ways sometimes, and when that time arrives, then they leave us for wherever 'tis they must go. All we may do thereon, it seems, is to partake of this lovely, cool forest and to think lovingly on them."

At his words, the dark wood did stir and whisper above the bent heads of the good and kind king and his belovèd queen.

Tale the Second
Clever Clyde

E'en as a wee lad, Clever Clyde loved outwitting others.

If butter was found upon a door handle or salt in a sugar bowl, certain sure could we be 'twas Clever Clyde's handiwork. One day, someone stirred white pepper into the dog's meat. The next, Baby's rattle was tied with twine fast to the cat's tail.

When Farmer Gleason and faithful Dobbin come down the back lane a-hauling a cart of hay, poor Dobbin did stumble over a rope stretched taut between two trees. Up popped a scarecrow clad in Clever Clyde's father's Sunday best. Whilst wheezing Dobbin cantered away, Farmer Gleason plucked himself up from the mire to the triumphant laughter of an ingenious lad.

One frigid December eve, someone poured water on

the steps of the old kirk. Such that, we worshippers fell to our knees on the morrow long before we reached the Communion Rail.

The eld Spinster Poole grew ever more stooped day by day—'til we found that someone had been hewing an inch a time off her crutch at night. Blind Dirk the seaman, home this twelve years upon the high seas, found his tin cup full, not of alms but of buttons, when went he into the Swan and Duck to buy his drop o' rum.

Still and all, Clever Clyde's dear mother, Doting Ingrid, could find no fault in her darling son. "He is, I ween, a high-spirited lad; but wot dost ye expect of such an intelligent child, a-growing up here in our sleepy hamlet?" With a mother's care, she ruffled Clever Clyde's golden locks and kissed his bronzed forehead. "When he grows to be a man, I 'spect he shall reflect brilliantly on us, one and all."

Thereto did Meek Frank, Clever Clyde's father, add with a slow shake of his head: "Aye. The ladies had best watch theirselves when our lad becomes a man!"

In due course, Clever Clyde, the mischievous lad, did grow into Clever Clyde, the sharp young man. Tall and willow lithe was he. His golden curls outshone the angels', and his eyes were blue as the welkin in June. Soon enow, did Clever Clyde leave our drowsy village to seek his fortune in the great world.

From time to time, we heard that Clever Clyde took a 'prenticeship—though had he never, in our ken, plied any trade—and that he acquired mastery. Thereafter, came word that Clever Clyde worked wonders. He took others' money and returned it to 'em tenfold in but a year and a day. By arts fair or foul, we decided, Clever Clyde was the summer sun that rose from our little village—just as Doting Ingrid had foretold.

None of us had e'er a spare penny to lend, of course. We be but humble folk, content to keep our farthings close in our pockets and our eyes on the task to hand. That did naught to save us from basking in Clever Clyde's reflected glory.

Soon, a gilt coach-and-four appeared upon our village square. Nor were we surprised to see Clever Clyde himself inside, smiling broad and bright as the August sun.

"Greetings, my dear and lowly friends," said he, stepping forth. "What pleasure it giveth me to be home here in my belovèd little village once again."

"Greetings to thee, Clever Clyde," mumbled we all.

"Good people, do I have an opportunity for ye!" Clever Clyde proclaimed. "In practically no time at all, and at absolutely no risk to ye, I shall multiply your pennies tenfold, as our Good Lord did multiply them loaves and fishes. Guaranteed. For I have studied at the feet of masters and am privy to their mighty arts."

Farmer Gleason muttered, "Incredible!" Blind Dirk groped for what coins were to be found in his tin cup. Spinster Poole spat out "Men!" as though the word were rotten fruit.

Then Doting Ingrid did speak aloud: "There's my bonny boy! Who wouldna trust so brilliant and so sharp a fellow? What a fine reflection is he on this village and on we, his proud parents!"

"Aye. And the ladies had best watch theirselves, also," observed Meek Frank.

Thus did Clever Clyde's parents carry the day, and anon the village entire, not excepting e'en Spinster Poole, lined up to 'vest in Clever Clyde's special scheme.

As he pocketed our pennies and our farthings one by one, Clever Clyde thought: "Am I not the sharpest, most brilliant young man this village has e'er—or e'er shall—see? How could this fine day dawn any better?"

At the end of the queue, patiently waited a dark Gypsy that nary a one of us had seen afore.

"Art thou Clever Clyde?" this stranger asked when, at last, she reached the head of the queue.

"Why, so I am," Clever Clyde replied with his grandest smile. "And who might thou be? I don't recall seeing thee afore in this village."

"Not likely, as I've ne'er been here afore," replied the eld woman. "Least ways not in this guise."

"Well, well, then; be that as it may. Hast thou a ducat or two to place in my little scheme?"

"Nay, lad. But I do have something else for thee."

"And what, my good woman, might that be?"

"A wish to come true," replied the Gypsy.

"A wish? But one wish? I thought it customary to grant three," said Clever Clyde with a knowing wink to us standing by.

"'Tis. 'Tis," the Gypsy admitted. "But thou be such a clever fellow that surely one wish will do thee well."

Now, 'tis a truth oft stated that those in the wish-granting business be slippery eels; and it should ha' been plain as a meat pie on a plate that the Gypsy had found Clever Clyde's Achilles' heel.

"She's right, thou knowst," mused Clever Clyde. "A man as bright and sharp as I can surely make one wish do for three."

"Well, then, what must I do to earn this wish-come-true?" queried he.

"Only return these good people's meager savings, and I will grant whatever thou wisheth."

"Done and done!" shouted Clever Clyde, his blue eyes shining eagerly.

When our pockets were once again as full of copper as ever they'd been, Clever Clyde turned to the eld woman. "Now then, thou must grant me my wish."

The Gypsy woman nodded, her arms crossed. Clever Clyde considered slyly and deduced that he could obtain all else he might e'er desire, if only he were sharper and more brilliant than the next man. "I wish henceforth," announced he, "to be even more bright and more sharp than already I am."

"And so shall thou be," grinned the Gypsy. "Poof!"

There before our very eyes in but an instant, Clever Clyde became a flaring mirror of glass, reflecting the brilliance of the noonday sun.

"What be this? Hold a minute," said the mirror.

"Yes?" smiled the Gypsy.

"I said I wished the more brilliant to be. This—why, 'tis nothing more than bad wordplay, not at all what I had in mind. Besides that, I don't feel a whit sharper."

"Ah. Right thou art. I had forgot," the Gypsy said. "Sharper it is, then."

And from beneath her colorful shawl, the crafty Old One drew forth a wee hammer of silver. With it, she tapped Clever Clyde into smithereens. Clever Clyde—or rather sharp shards of him—lay scattered about the green, reflecting the brilliance of the sun into our gawping faces.

"Yikes!" said Farmer Gleason.

"What happened?" asked Blind Dirk.

"Men!" spat out Spinster Poole.

"I'd best go fetch a broom," said Meek Frank morosely. "Ladies, ye must watch thyselves, what with all this broken glass lying about."

Tale the Third
Ballad of the Fifth Bairn

"**O Mother dear**," keened Wycroft, young and wan, "whate'er shalt I do? For I do pine all grievously, yet she knows not my pain."

"Soft now, my blue-eyed son," soothed Mother Patience low. "For all doth know how deep true love's waters do run. 'Twere better to another thou did cleave, whence true love shalt come whilst thou but watch and wait."

Yet, smitten sore was Wycroft—and smitten had he been since the day the hairs did sprout upon his dewy chin.

Then, "Father dear," did woeful Wycroft sigh; "whate'er shalt I do? 'Tis sure I die if I can't speak of what my heart doth hold. Yet, what if she should harken not—or hearing, just say 'no?'"

"Be bold, my fond and foolish boy," replied his father,

Will. "For moaning heart did ne'er win the lovely lady fair. And, many be the silver fish that swim the silver seas. Go to and find another—and let me eat this cod in peace."

But willful Wycroft would not go, nor would he fish the seas. No, he stood fast, a graveyard stone, on which was "Prudence" 'graven.

"Is my love not a flow'r that blooms be-dewèd in the morning sun? Why stoops she not to breathe it in or pluck its blossoms bright? And why, whene'er we two meet, doth this, my agile tongue, turn then and there to lead, and my mouth fill up with sand?"

These and many words alike did wretched Wycroft groan, as through in the vaulted heaven above, the sun and stars and moon their senseless courses ran.

This while as well, did Prudence grow as many lasses will, with all her wits about her wary and both eyes watchful wide.

Thought she, "Someday shalt I find love—or mayhap, 'twill find me. Yet, Cupid doth a bandage wear and shoots his honeyed arrows blind. That so, more watchful must I be, for many be the fish that swim about the silver sea, nor doth a faint heart well avail a maid."

In sooth, was Prudence fair, the fairest in our dale. Like freshet waters in the spring, her copper tresses coursed. As meadows green were her clear eyes; as the sapling's, was her grace. All ripe to taste appeared her cherry lips and dainty were her ears. As sweet as mead, or so they say, was ev'ry breath she breathed. Who would his heart not lose to a such lass as this?

About her, swains did swarm as bees 'bout fresh windfall. Ruddy Rod offer'd sugared sonnets, both English and Italian. Lame Larry proffered wilting posies, whilst

Auld Alfred on market day jangled golden coins near about her ears. E'en Laird Birdbower did chat her up nor minded not the dour frowns of his sour lady, Vigilance.

Only Wycroft—only he—did hold himself aloof. What if, feared he, he should proclaim his love and she his tender suit deny? What then? Nay, 'twas best to stand aside and gain whate'er reward a loyal heart, though silent still, might gain.

Should Prudence glimpse her lover when through the town she trod, why, then would Wycroft dart into the chandler's shop, or in the alehouse door, or crouch like a frightened coney within the hedgerows thick beside the village lane. From thence, should Prudence dwell upon his furtive deeds, 'twould cause her wary heart to shudder.

And so, did years and days roll by, as days and years do roll; and pragmatic Pru did love find—or mayhap love found her. Upon a Thursday bright, were she and Ernst wed. Handsome was he and great of foot and frame, yet as earnest as a child. Handsome and stout came forth their children four; and snug they dwelt in the cottage Ernst had built, safe and snug behind his cottage door.

These things did steadfast Wycroft stand, still faithful to his Pru. Paid he the scullery maid no heed, so forward in her mien, nor heard he Wanda's bawdy hints, who toiled in the barn. Coy were the blandishments of Widow Wildroot, yet rolled they off Wycroft's mind as waves that lave a stone. Nor paused he e'en a jot when Hapless Hanna lay at his feet, a-moaning she must have him or she'd die. No, Wycroft stepped o'er her writhing form with but a weary sigh.

Spin as the world doth spin, and on their lives did go. Came chill or rain, wind or snow, by light of day or pitch of night, there Wycroft stood upon the cliffs high o'er the moaning seas. And there he wailed of his long love that only here he spoke. "The polar star doth shine above, so shines my purest love. Yet, still I find my fear too strong, now she be happ'ly wed—what boots my dear love now—and what becomes of me?"

And here might cease this ballad sad, had weary hearts not foundered. For, Wycroft learnt the dire news his Pru was great with child.

"O mother dear," mourns Wycroft now, "all hope is lost and gone. Her stolid husband might she flee were she my love to know. And surely, she would lightly leave her stoutish babes four! But five? Such happiness shalt ne'er be mine. Do, thou, make up my bed, for now my love is but a weighty stone, too burdensome to shift alone."

"Pluck up, my blue-eyed child, pluck up," scolds Mother Patience then, though sight and tresses both had now grown dull. "None die of broken hearts these days—'tis something just not done!"

"She's right, my tiresome lad," pipes up old Father Will. "Pray, end thy tedious tale, and I'll go fetch the lady fair—soon as I down this tranche o' cod. Then canst thou fill her dainty ears with noble sentiments and dreams."

Into his bed, wan Wycroft climbs, and to the wall turns he his face. Whereon he etches yet one last mark to the tally of his lifelong love.

Anon, stands patient Pru by his bedside, and great with child is she. "They say, dear man, that thou shalt die, and die thou shalt for me. Good sir, bestir thee not, for I shall lean in close," says she.

Now Wycroft feels the hand of Death, cold upon his chest; and now, at last, his tongue is loosed, and at the last, pours forth his woe. It speaks of the flower that blooms, regarding not the season; how like a guiding star love shines, despite the storm-tossed seas.

"My dearest love," sighs he at last, "long ha' I kept this hidden: I have loved thee and thee alone, though I was feared to say. Nor doubt I now my love shall last long after I be stilled."

Puzzled is Pru to hear all this, for six words only through the years hath she heard from him—and those be these: "Prithee, Maid, may I now pass?" And, is not Ernst the gentlest of men? And, does she not dote on Mattie, Ralph, May, and Little Lew?

With care doth kind Pru ponder what comfort she dares give. An easy lie 'twould be to say she loves him, too, so to his grave a happy man he goes. But what if he should revive a-sudden? For many do turn their faces to the wall at night just to awake the morning next, fresh as cowslips in that morning's light.

At length, Pru whispers both soft and low: "Dear man; thy steadfast love I hail, for few these days do love so firm and long as thou. Yet, I fear 'tis thy heart's pain thou now doth cherish, not me, the maid thou dost not know.

"And more: not I—nor any maiden fair or foul—dares love as ye men do. 'Tis true our hearts do fly as free as thine; yet we must not follow whereat they tend. Maids must love where love we might, not where'er we may. These days we wait like wary flowers, as down the lane come wanton lads, with heedless boots and switches cruel, our blooms perchance to spoil.

"Sorry am I to preach a lesson this hard. But, such have I seen and such have I learned—would that it were otherwise."

With pensive mien and troubled heart, doth Prudence quit his deathbed now. Nor looks she back, but wends her way back to her cottage door.

"Right fair is she, the fairest in our dell," says Father Will in awe. "Small wonder Wycroft loved her so and loves her still, it seems."

"And right practical is she, too," Mother Patience growls, her eye upon her gawping man. "Had she but spake thus to our lad these many years ago, what sorrows 'twould ha' spared!"

Keen blow the winds over the cliffs where constant Wycroft lies. Shrill call the birds that fall and rise high in those wind-whipped skies. *Now or Never. Never or Now* is that of which they sing.

Before a cottage door, four stout children play; and "Wycroft" is the name a newborn bairn now bears. Within that cottage dim at night, doth stolid Ernst muse: why would his Prudence so grand a name give so meek a child?

Tale the Fourth
Truth and the Maiden

Let village greybeards debate whether Nurture or Nature is to blame; for we have seen that every bairn born into this world comes freighted with a character that shapes its fate.

So is it that Plain Hanna throws herself, o'er and o'er again, at the feet of heedless swains who love her not. So it is that Hideous Carl revels still in the cruelty that marred his brutish childhood, and Clyde delights in baffling all others. Or Ernst, most gentle and handsome 'tis true, is to this day as earnest slow as his wife, fair Prudence, is quick.

Sooth be said, we prefer it this way. It keeps life sorted and simple, and leaves us at liberty to mind fold and flock and field.

Now, once it fell out that there dwelt among us a lass of stone-steady honesty. "Truthful Vera" was she called;

and, from her infant speech (*Dada, you smell like goats.*) to that of her fifteenth year (*Mother, the hue of this costly shawl thou gaveth me flatters not mine hair nor mine eyes.*), Vera spoke only the truth, nor held she back a jot.

Some in our village surmised 'twas due to curse upon her doting parents, Goatherd Giles and Melinda the Mild, by Portentia, the crone whose forest hut sits near to their odorous goat farm. Others averred 'twas but a gift from a kindly godmother, now dwelling in Brussels. One opined Melinda and Giles had etched too soon upon a tender mind the value of unvarnished truth; while another swore her parents had punished the wee lass o'er harshly for but a childish lie or two.

Whether the cause was curse or gift or early lesson gone awry, the years flowed on, and Truthful Vera grew into an angular maid, striding amongst us like a reaper in a hectare of ripe corn. Straight as a sapling towered she, with truth flashing from her eyes and perched like a hunter's falcon upon her scythe of a tongue.

Whate'er the cause, there was one thing no one gainsaid of Truthful Vera: enough was enough. Few among us failed to shift our course or dodge into a doorway were we to spy her in our path. By the eve of her sixteenth year, Vera had sorely offended both high and low alike.

"My good Lord Mayor," she once announced, "know thou thy sons find thee a pompous windbag and would rather be wandering minstrels poor ere they'd follow in thy footsteps?"

"My dear Spinster Poole," she addressed that agèd one, "you do realize, do you not, that by appearing as though you be sucking on a lemon, you kill all hope of finding friend or lover or e'en a pet?"

To Wise Old Johan, who now sat pondering the ways of the world on his bench before the Swan and Duck, she did say: "Why people do account thee wise, I knoweth not. All I ha' e'er heard from thee amounts to ale-addled stuff and nonsense."

More, upon meeting Dame Molly on the high road of a summer's afternoon, Truthful Vera was so moved to point out: "Aye, paint and powder as thou wilt, Milady, but thy age and love of port wine shines through like stones in a freshet brook."

She told kind Ernst his earnestness was "boooring." His Prudence, she told that true love had passed her by, ne'er mind all her wary care. She informed the Village Elders they lacked vision; and one Sunday morning, she pronounced to Parson Wooltyne that his sermons had all the redemptive force of a seaside snail.

"Thou art so very vain," Truthful Vera said to Preston the Glorious, even though the village girls hung about this glittering youth like hungry cats at the butcher's door. "Thou art but a strumpet and a whore, I fear," Vera announced to the barmaid Polly, who had, 'til that day, thought of herself more as a fount of solace for the lost, the lonely, and the distraught.

Vera told the village children their lives would fill with disappointment after disappointment and they'd best get used to it now. E'en to me, the humble teller of this tale, Truthful Vera did say, "Thou'll never get published, thou knowest."

In sum and in all, Truthful Vera did spare none, neither small nor great.

Giles and Melinda tried in vain to school their daughter

in the art of a tactful lie; or, failing that, in the prudence of sage silence.

Unto which teaching Truthful Vera would hector: "Oh, ye purblind parents! Loathe am I to utter platitudes and false praises, no matter how some long to hear 'em. Nor can I sit all stony silent whilst others prance about like fools. We durst not allow self-deception to flower, but must root it out, face the truth bravely and act thereon as we should." And strode she forth from their humble cot, more upright and stiffer of spine than e'er.

"Oh, she's a hard-un, that girl," sighed Goatherd Giles sadly.

"She hath a point, nonetheless," replied Melinda meekly, "though 'tis sheathed in words, 'tis sharp as a sabre."

Now, it came to pass, on the eve of Vera's birthday, that the Village Elders met in secret session.

"Something must be done and soon," announced the Lord Mayor. "In sooth, we can no longer handle the truth, nor abide with it flowing like a torrent in spring all freely among us."

While Old Johan sat a-puzzling how one could dwell 'midst truth and yet be unable to abide it, the other Village Elders nodded their agreements as sagely as they could.

"'Tis terrible true, your Lordship," murmured Alfred the Affirmer. "Well put, in truth."

"Yet, what then may we do?" asked Elder Eckbar. "For the child hath a will stronger than iron and a spine more unbending than the sturdiest of oaks."

"Mayhap there be one that can aid us in this, our hour of need," intoned the Mayor. "And I, shouldering the weighty cloak of mayordom, have reached forth to this person—at great personal danger to myself and my family, might I add! Oh, how heavy sits the mayor's velvet cap 'pon the head of he that wears it! And, oh, how do these perilous times call for courage of heart, and the wisdom to. . ."

"Er, your Honor?" interjected Elder Eckbar. "Forgive me, but 'tis not yet election year, nor be there villagers here enow to applaud thy heroic sacrifice. Tell us, prithee: who be this mysterious personage?"

"Ahem. Yes. Well. I have asked her to join us this evening, in the expected event of thy acquiescence," amended the Lord Mayor. And, from behind a curtain, stepped the forest crone.

"Let us not shilly-shally," said this old one brusquely. "I'm a woman what needs her sleep, and the night air suits me ill. Well am I acquainted with thy dilemma, and I know what ye fain would do if do you could."

"Oh, but do nothing drastic," piped up Elder Timid Thomas. "We want none injured nor impaired."

"Ye know the rules as well as I," the crone replied. "It lies not within my powers to alter the basics of our human natures, nor dare I snuff out the brief, bright candle of life. We are what we are, sooth to say, and so must we remain 'til our appointed hour."

"What of education?" muttered Old Johan. "What of reclamation, what of renewal?" But, as usual, no one paid him the slightest heed.

Whilst the good Elders chewed upon their visitor's limitations, the Lord Mayor asked, "What then dost thou propose?"

"Bring the girl unto the village commons tomorrow at noon precisely, and ye shall see." Whereupon in a puff of azure smoke, the eld woman was gone.

What could our Village Elders do then but that which Village Elders have always done? At noon, they, Truthful Vera, her doting parents, and the village entire gathered on the village commons.

Portentia awaited us there, leaning on her stick, 'neath the shade of its ancient yew.

"Truthful Vera," said this beldame, "I ask of thee now whether or no thou wilt henceforth add but a little leavening of lies to the hard crust of truth."

"In truth, dusky one, I prefer not. 'Tis my nature to pass this life with my eyes open wide and to speak of foolishness and folly whene'er I see it, whate'er it be. I was born a truth-teller and a truth-teller always shalt I be," said the bold lass, her head high and her eyes ablaze.

Thereat, the crone leaned in close to the proud young lady and whispered in her ear. Slowly, Vera looked up to where the sky rests upon the edge of the earth, then nodded and softly said, "As thou doth wish, so do I desire."

"As so thou chooseth," said the crone. "With the powers vested in me by the spirits of our somber, drear forest and the Elders of this village, I hereby enact the will of ye, one and all, and of His Honor, the Lord Mayor."

Immediately, Vera felt her spine stiffen e'en more and her unblinking gaze become more fixed upon the distant hills. All trace of doubt or confusion left her, and her heart grew still as stone.

Where once a strapping girl of sixteen had stood, there was erected now an obelisk of white marble, hewn from the hills of Carrara. *Veritas* was writ upon its base, and at its tip blazed a pure, eternal flame.

"My goodness," said Meek Melinda. "What hast thou

done?"

"Only what ye required of me," replied the crone brusquely.

"She speaks the truth, dear mother," said the obelisk hollowly. "For now see I more clearly than e'er before and now I stand here at ready whene'er truth needs be told."

As time passed, to speak true, fewer and fewer villagers consulted Vera, our smoldering pillar of truth. That we were not really, truly loved; that we lacked the talent we thought we had; that others flattered us to our faces and sniggered behind our backs—all seemed to matter less and less as time went by.

Still and all, *Veritas* did become a pilgrim's shrine of sorts, and our village did thrive upon those who thronged to our marble obelisk to hear the unpolished truth, if only for once in their lives. . .

. . . after which, they retreated to the Swan and Duck, where in dim, smoky corners, they chewed solemnly on the bitter crust of knowledge Vera had dished out to them.

Tale the Fifth
Belovèd Gemma

Upon a time not so long ago, an elderly king and his queen ruled their tiny kingdom on the far side of the deep, drear forest. King Francisco and Queen Magdalena were generous and kind, and their devotion to one another was cause enow for the undying love and pride of their subjects.

Yet, one thing sat heavy upon their royal hearts. Try as they might, Magdalena brought forth no royal child. Now the queen's hair was turning grey and, of late, the king took care to see that his jeweled crown sat square o'er the bald spot on his pate before he left the Royal Bedchamber.

Nor was this mere vanity. Rather, they wished heartily to spare their subjects worry over what might befall the kingdom once they were gone.

Then, a miracle occurred: Queen Magdalena found herself with child. In a trice did King Francisco send for the wisest heads in the kingdom—which, in truth, were not that many—and they all urged the happy queen to quaff plenty of fluids and elevate her Regal Feet throughout the day.

This Magdalena faultlessly did; and, in due course, she brought forth into the world a healthy baby girl.

"She is beautiful, my dear," said King Francisco; "near as beauteous to mine eyes as thee thyself." And tenderly he caressed the queen's weary cheek.

"She is our most precious possession," agreed the queen, "not unlike the prime jewel in your ancient crown. I would that we name her Princess Gemma therefore." And good Queen Magdalena stroked tenderly the fresh, pink cheek of their little princess.

In those days, word of a Royal Birth spread far, fast, and wide; and sooner rather than later, appeared an agèd crone at cradle-side.

"Hold fast, old woman!" cried Queen Magdalena. "I would not have thee pass along foul pestilence nor sniffle to our priceless princess."

"Guards!" bellowed King Francisco. "Guards!"

As Sergeants Sven and Ricardo lumbered in, the old crone said: "Fear me not, I beg of thee, for I have et my herbs and elixirs all, and most careful am I of the night air. Nay, here I be merely to bless this long-awaited bairn and speak of her future."

"Pray, say on then and be done withal," quoth Queen Magdalena, while grave Caution and rash Curiosity sang a roundelay in her wits.

"I can but see darkly, as well ye know; yet for the

Princess Gemma I foresee a life o'er ruled by love. In sooth, see I a love as hard and as bright as diamonds."

"Be it so," said the king, "and then be our princess truly blessed. Guards, see ye this rheumy-eyed one out, and take good care she tumbles not into the moat."

Sven and Ricardo followed the king's command without demure, and in good time, the infant princess grew straight and strong into a child, and thence a young woman of extraordinary beauty.

Queen Magdalena and King Francisco, the while, grew ever more stooped, and the king developed a tremor in his right hand that made wielding his scepter ever more difficult by the day. E'en so, the devotion of the old couple to their brilliant child impressed us all. Queen Magdalena loved her only daughter as the wind loves the trees; and, as for the love King Francisco held for Princess Gemma, why 'twas beyond all simile.

In all, the princess wanted for naught. Her chamber overflowed with the finest silks, the brightest jewels, and most novel beauty potions from the East, both Near and Far. The doting king and queen made certain Gemma lacked not for fresh fruit nor vegetables, no matter what the season; and, whenever the princess desired a chocolate éclair or mulberry popover, the Royal Kitchen sprung into action forthwith.

Should a clever village lad invent an ingenious gadget, Princess Gemma would be the first in her kingdom to own it. She had her own gilt carriage with a brace of gleaming, black steeds. When she took up archery, King Francisco had crafted for her a bow of burnished gold. When she ventured an interest in watercolors, Queen Magdalena brought in a master from Provence as her tutor. In short and in sum, Princess Gemma wanted for nothing, as befits one of her esteemed lineage and beauty.

Most of all, the princess ne'er doubted the steadfast love of the old queen and king. Each night, they tucked her into her silken bed with kisses and prayers. Each morning, they greeted her with kisses and eager queries about her hopes for the new day. If, as it sometimes befell, their attentions felt a little o'ermuch, Princess Gemma had merely to cast her violet eyes over the many signs of their unrestraint and think, "'Tis but a small price to pay. Where else could I find another palace so walled about and so plastered snug with love?"

Thus did all things stand when, on a day, Count Brewster, the most trusted, loyal and longest-serving of counselors, did come to the king and queen's Retiring Chamber during an ebb in the stream of humble petitioners and wronged litigants.

"My dear King Francisco and my belovèd Queen Magdalena," croaked this old count. "Far be it from me to tell ye how to rule thy kingdom . . . yet I wonder if ye ha' considered the dear Princess Gemma's future. She is, as ye doubtless have perceived, approaching the age of matrimony, and there be whispers in some obscure corners of the realm that Princess Gemma is not that way inclined."

"Trouble thy grey head no further," said the queen, peering in Count Brewster's general direction. "We are aware of the situation and anon will act 'pon it."

"Indeed," chimed in King Francisco, "we have the matter firmly fixed in our Royal Minds."

Of course, they did not. Indeed, the very thought that Princess Gemma might—in truth *must*—wed and produce an heir made the Royal Pair most ill at ease.

That night in the Royal Bedchamber, Queen Magdalena said with rue: "What must be done, must needs be done. I suppose all princesses be given in marriage at some time or t'other. 'Twas my fate—and good fortune to be sure—and while I love her like mine own self, it must be the Princess Gemma's end as well." Hereat deeply sighed the queen.

"Mayhap, it must be done as thou sayst," replied the king. "Ne'ertheless, it must be done with extreme care. Loathe am I to offer up my beloved jewel to just any Johan-Come-Recently that pranceth through our palace gates." For, if the queen's love for her dear daughter was as the corn is for the sun, the king's love was beyond compare.

"*Our* jewel, meanest thou," Queen Magdalena corrected. "She is our child, and our child must she remain. We shall not give her away; more like we but loan her for a time to the most suitable of lords."

"And the terms of that loan shall be beyond imagining," said the king gruffly.

Thus it came to pass that word went out, far and near: the beautiful and charming Princess Gemma was on the market, a prize made doubly attractive by the advanced age of her loving parents. In the blink of an eye, suitors descended upon the little kingdom beyond the wood like a pack of ravening wolves upon a flock of helpless lambs.

And, what a pack of suitors were they!

Here came Lord Angular from the next kingdom but one, who was six foot nine if he be but an inch, and moved as though plied by puppet strings. Here came the warty Earl Walters, of whom little more needs be said. There was Prince Stan, the Stutterer; the Viscount Hysteria (who could not stop talking save when he gulped for air); and the Grand Duke Ralph the Ever Ready, who was far and away too eager to please.

From the dark forest itself came Lord Vladimir, whose long, black beard failed to conceal a perpetual scowl as he gobbled both meat and fowl from the lavish suitors' board King Francisco and Queen Magdalena laid out each midday. The incomparably handsome Lord Lionel knew just how to stand so that his magnificent profile and crispèd hair showed to best advantage. And, from where or how no one quite knew, appeared a tragic, little hunchback, who offered the princess naught but a spinning wheel and pile of golden straw.

In truth, did each and all bring the princes gifts: fine shawls from skilled Welch weavers, exotic spices from the Indies, rare pearls in ornate boxes, and gift baskets of wine, chocolate, and theatre tickets.

King Francisco eyed each new suitor with distaste and fear. This one was too old; that one too poor; another was too superficial. As best he could, he slyly observed Princess Gemma. Did she seem to favor this one over that? Did her violet eyes brighten when one suitor or another came nigh? Did she laugh over-much at that one's jest or lean in to whisper a *bon mot* to this other?

Of a midnight weary, after another long, dull day of suitors on parade, the old couple laid their heads to rest upon their silken pillows. But sleep would not come.

Instead, their bed-chamber door opened and in tiptoed Princess Gemma.

"My dear, dear parents," the shivering princess began. "I fear that I must talk to ye or I shall die."

"Oh my goodness," said King Francisco, bolting

upright in the Royal Bed. "Do climb in and warm thyself ere thou catch thy death of chill."

Once so settled, Princess Gemma heaved a sigh both loud and long. "I do appreciate all that ye are doing to help me find a suitable suitor, indeed I do," she said. "Alas, I find my heart is not in it. In truth, each and every one of them leaves me colder and colder inside, and as a group— well . . ." and here the princess shuddered.

"But, my darling daughter," said Queen Magdalena, "having suitors and selecting a husband one day is the lot and burden of all good princesses."

"And yet," said King Francisco thoughtfully, "there is no point in wedging one's foot into a shoe that doth not fit, so to say. If the suitors do not suit, may we not put an end to this charade anon?"

A brown study fell over the Royal Family for a time.

Then King Francisco brightened. "Mayhap there is someone who can help us. I shall send for her at once."

Later that same starless night, in the dim hours before dawn, three figures trod with care out across the Royal Drawbridge that spanned the Royal Moat. To the blear eyes of the sleepy guards, they seemed but an eld crone in a dark shawl leading Sven and Ricardo, both nearly blind themselves, back toward the forest, deep and drear.

In the days thereafter, nowhere could the Princess Gemma be found. In little time, did her suitors lose patience for prowling about the little castle, for little there was, other than a sumptuous luncheon, to hold their interest; and anon they, too, faded away like a sunny morning's dew.

Soon as well, speculation among the courtiers and sage counselors dwindled to a mere trickle, as the peaceful little kingdom settled back into its drowsy routine.

"Fear I, My Lord," said Count Brewster one exceptionally dull afternoon, "that when we are no longer, our kingdom must pass to your nephew, the Lord Duke Owen the Odious."

"That 'tis as that will be," shrugged King Francisco. "Are we not, after all, but a tiny kingdom and hardly sustainable in these times?"

"Besides," observed Queen Magdalena, "Owen's not so bad. I hear tell he has some wonderful schemes to make agriculture more profitable for both the landholders and their serfs."

Count Brewster grew quiet for a moment, pondering this new indifference. "By-the-by, My Lord," he then observed, "remiss would I be were I not to compliment you upon the new jewel that sits so prominently and shines forth so radiantly in your crown. It is a thing of rare beauty, and, I ween, extremely precious."

At the old count's observation, the rare gem in the King's Crown sparkled brightly in a beam of sunlight, and Queen Magdalena gazed long and lovingly on it. The old king raised a trembling hand and caressed the glorious jewel that gleamed so proudly there. It was a caress that many at court had observed him perform often of late.

Some say, too, a salt tear slid from the queen's eye as she gazed upon the old king in his bejeweled crown. Although I must add that, in those days, few of us were as sharp of vision and quick of thought as in our youth.

Tale the Sixth
The Woodsman's Fair Children

In times before memories begin, there dwelt an old woman, with only a dog and cat for her companions, in a mean cottage deep within the forest. O'ergrown was the path to her cottage door, and long had woody vines twined o'er her humble home's walls and roof.

Some said she was a witch, who sailed abroad at moonrise astride a broom of straw. Others sniffed and said, "Posh and nonsense! She be but a wiccan—mayhap a tad awry inside her head." A few opined e'en that she was but a mad poet, for late into the pitch of night was she oft glimpsed scribbling away at her sheaf of foolscap.

Whate'er their view, nary a one durst utter a word of greeting when the old woman appeared at market, such was their awe and fear of her.

In truth, the old woman preferred things that way.

From the very day that her poor lover, D'Anton the Dyslexic, turned himself into a newt (through an unfortunate confusion over the hieroglyphics of an obscure Coptic spell), the eld woman sought solace in thoughts of days gone by—and in the company of her pets—beside the dying embers of her hearth fire. Indeed, she bestowed upon those twain the power of speech, so that her nights might not seem so long nor so empty.

Of a morning, whilst their owner was to village market, that same cat and dog did open their hearts to one another thus:

"For myself, well-a-weary be I of all her hoary tales of days a-gone," lazily yawned the cat. "Sore do I fear our agèd Mistress hath grown forgetful, as we must list to the same stories o'er and o'er again."

"Thinkest thou so?" said the dog, gnawing on a tattered slipper. "I pay no heed. Once Mistress starts her nightly murmuring and mumbling and scribbling things down, why, 'tis a simple matter to catch a wink or two."

"That be because all thou doth do is utter 'lovely' betwixt thy snores," hissed the cat. "Fie; 'tis time we took matters betwixt our own two paws. I be in grievous need of evening rest; nor do I wish to hear yet again of Mistress's wedding trip to Sicily."

"Oh, but that be one of my favorite tales," protested the dog. "I do dearly love the bit about the lava flow."

"What a literal-minded beast thou art," sighed the cat. "But hark now, I have a plan. Come the morrow, we two shall sally forth into the forest wide to seek fit company for Mistress, someone that shall spare us the onus and burthen of listening."

"Prithee, wouldst thou go o'er that but once again?"

quoth the dog. "I doubt I am clear on all the details."

The cat did once more repeat her plan—more slowly this time—and so their plot was hatched.

Each and every day thereafter did the cat and dog roam the dusky forest, interviewing all manner of creatures, small and great. It proved a most discouraging quest, for few of the forest dwellers rated high for sociability and fewer still could sustain a conversation.

Then one day, just as the dog was once again losing focus, the two animals heard voices. Near, in a shadowy glade stood a blond girl and a blond boy dressed in humble peasants' weeds. As the cat and dog watched, the girl carefully plucked a crumb of bread from her basket and placed this crumb upon the ground.

"There; that should aid us to find our way home when comes the time, dear brother," said she.

"Soon enough shall they rue the day they decided to wed, I daresay," swore the lad. "And then, they shall welcome us home with tears and sweet treats; and whate'er we wish thenceforth shall be their commandment."

"Greetings" said the cat, stepping into the clearing. "By any chance, might ye be seeking a place to eat and mayhap rest thy weary heads?"

"*Gott im Himmel!*" exclaimed the girl; "a talking cat!"

"I, too, have that skill," offered up the dog. "'Tis just that nothing in particular springs to mind on the moment."

"To speak the truth, we *do* be rather hungry and thirsty," confessed the boy. "Where lies this refuge or haven thou speaketh of?"

So it was that when the old woman returned home

from market, she found the dog, the cat, the boy, and the girl enjoying a bowl of cream and strawberries and bread and playing at skittles—a pastime for which the dog and cat were not so well suited, as ye can imagine.

"I ween ye must stay the night," replied the old woman, after hearing the children's piteous 'plaint. "And whereas I've come from market, so shall we have good things to eat, at least this one eve."

By the time the children were well sated, bathed and had completed their prayers, 'twas the pitch of night and the great forest then was whispering its ancient tales. The old woman, the dog and the cat settled round their dwindling fire.

"'Tis true enow," began the old woman. "Of late have I felt the chill tide of loneliness flow and ebb about my heart, and these children ye ha' found be, to all appearances, clean and polite. Tish; they e'en remembered me in their prayers. But, certain sure they belong to somebody, as most kinder do; and we canna keep 'em here long. They will eat us out of cot and home."

"Lovely," murmured the dog, who was dozing. "The lad is a wonder at stick-tossing, and the girl knows just where to scratch behind mine ears."

"I trust having them here will not interfere with my naps," worried the cat, who had not fully foreseen the cost of the children's upkeep ere now.

"They must stay with us until we can find their parents," said the old woman "Come, let us enjoy what little sleep we can. 'Tis well past first watch, and on the morrow we must again see to our guests."

In this manner did these fair children bide with the old woman, the dog and the cat, one day and then the next.

Gently, as the summer breeze doth make the grasses sing and the hedgerows murmur, did the old woman draw forth their story from the easeful boy and girl.

"Our father has married himself to a wicked, evil stepmother," confessed the blond girl one day. "And hard against us hath she turned his heart."

"Aye," added the lad wistfully; "as fair and loving as our dear mother was, she is both harsh and cruel."

Another day but one, the boy observed: "Loathe would we be to leave thee, dear old hag, for thou asketh naught of us save that we be lively and of good appetite. Our wicked stepmother wanted us to carry water and make up our pallets and lay out our clothes."

Once, as the children feasted on rice pudding with cinnamon and sugar (the old woman's specialty), the girl observed, "Our wicked stepmother would oft make us dine on cabbage, broccoli, or cauliflower."

"And fruit," chimed in the boy. "She made us eat one apple each day!"

Well the old woman knew that loss of a doting mother lingers long, like the crusted snow that sometimes sleeps still in the fens and fells all through June. So, too, had she, in her time, heard many a tale told of the wickedness of stepmothers. "Yet, such tales and the truth do oft take separate paths," thought she.

Then, whilst gathering mushrooms for the children's evening omelet, the old woman espied a woodsman who dwelt at the forest verge. Beside him walked a raven-haired woman in apron and dirndl, with bright eyes and a pale face. High and low, this mournful pair helloed, as they trudged through the darkening, tangled wood.

"We must return here the morrow and here resume

our tedious search," quoth the worthy woodsman wearily.

"Nor must we must e'er give in nor give up," insisted the wretched woman, placing her hand softly upon his powerful arm. "We must find them and fetch them home."

At that very instant did the old woman know what she must do.

That selfsame eve, as the fair-haired boy and sweet-faced girl snored softly under the old woman's feather bolster, she laid out her plan before the cat and the dog.

"Mistress, we shall do just as thou asketh," said the cat. "If we play our parts well, things shall be as once they were, and I can return to my morning naps and my evening bowls of fresh milk."

"I doubt I quite understand the plan aright," apologized the dog. So the old woman related yet again—this time more slowly—what it was that each of them must say and do.

The morning next, up sat the fair-haired boy and rubbed the sleep from his sky-blue eyes. "I fancy honey pancakes this morning, dear hag," he called out.

"With gooseberry jam and fine sugar atop," added the sweet-faced girl, her golden locks all a-tumble about her rosy cheeks. "I have slept long and well and fain would eat anon."

But the old woman merely continued bustling about the little cottage as if her ears were made of wood.

Then said the cat, staring at the children with her golden eyes large and shining: "As you may well see, our Mistress is very busy this morning of all mornings. 'Twill prove a very special day for us all." The cat's pink tongue licked her lips and she grinned hideously.

In wonder the boy and the girl watched as the old

woman kindled a roaring fire in her oven and assembled a chef's array of herbs, spices and glittering knives upon her oaken carving block.

"What be so special about this day of all days?" queried the girl.

"Oh, I canna tell thee that," said the cat. "'Twould spoil the surprise, would it not?" With a glance in the dog's direction, the cat curled up in the beam of sun that poured in through the open cottage door.

"I do like surprises," said the boy. "They almost always bring me things I have desired; and when they do not, they be, belike, things I've not yet known I did desire."

"Maybe not this time," the dog piped up on cue. "For with this day comes a fine feast for some here—them what have labored to feed and entertain ye. But ne'er ye mind. Mayhap I have said too much too soon."

The boy and girl looked at each other with their four blue eyes wide. Then they looked at the old woman, who was grinding the blade of an enormous cleaver, sharp as sharp may be.

By the cottage doorway, the cat opened one golden eye as the two children tiptoed hastily by. "More cream for me, I ween," she thought as out the door and into the forest they fled.

"Pray dear, follow them and see that they find their way along the bread crumbs I have laid, back to the clearing where, *sans* doubt, their father and stepmother will greet them with loving arms and kisses aplenty," the old woman told the dog. "I must put this fire out, for it promises to be a warm day."

The dog followed these instructions faithfully, as dogs will.

"That went well," observed the cat, casually licking her velvet paw.

"Aye," said the old woman. "They were not bad children, as children go. And, I am certain sure they shall, as children do, craft a tale to account for their whereabouts—a tale, I fear, 'twill cast dark and sinister shadows o'er all our deeds and cares."

"Making themselves look all the cleverer, too, I ween," purred the cat.

"Doubt it not," replied the old woman ruefully. "Suspicious hearts in the village will turn e'en harder 'gainst me. Ah well, mayhap 'tis not all in vain. Of late have I been thinking of marketing in the next village o'er but one, where I hear the Trader Johan has opened a fine, new shop, well stocked with goods from the world o'er."

"And fish?" asked the cat.

"Bones for the dog and fish fresh from the deep, wide sea for thee, my dear," replied the crone with a kindly smile.

Tale the Seventh
The Chanson of Constance and Franklin

At sundown on a fine September eve, the Silver Swan set sail; and there did Seaman Franklin stand, a-lingering at the rail. He bid his Constance fair a fond farewell, whilst she did bide upon the shore—long past when all the wives and children had unto their suppers gone.

Stood Constance there well past the hour the Swan's proud sails did fade, like stars that dim when comes the dawn. Then cried she out o'er the ocean's roil: "Return, my love, and safe thy coming home may be, by dark or day, in summer or in snow; for thee shalt I be waiting."

The shoreline smudge below the sea's sharp rim had long dropped down ere Seaman Franklin left the Swan's rough rail. "And when shalt mine eyes feast once more on my Constance dear? And when shalt we embrace once more in pleasant dell or lea? 'Tis down to Tide and Time to tell," wearily sighed he.

Then up spoke Agèd Albert; the eldest mariner he: "A fond and foolish lad thou art to moon as doth a young sea calf! 'Twill boot thee naught. For long ere we return—if return we do from off these per'lous seas—thy Constance shalt another ha' found and to her thou shalt be no more than the burnt up wick of a guttered candle stick."

"Say ye so, and so say you all?" young Franklin asked the Swan's rough crew. The "Ayes" and "So 'tises" and "By the Lord Harrys" that answer'd back were like a chorus of ravens black.

"Come, me lads; put your backs now to it," cried the quartermaster grave. "We've distant lands and ventures new in distant seas to brave."

Still young Franklin kept his amour close, clasped fast within a locket gold that ne'er left his breast, wherein lay tresses cut with care and blessed by Constance fair.

Far sailed the Silver Swan o'er seas uncharted to lands as yet unnamed. At times the seas were meadows green, and all that dwelt therein did sport beside the hissing hull.

At times the waters were as mountains wild that toss'd the Swan unto the sun ere dashing her to the depths, a fall so swift that the saltiest tar, e'en he, retched up his rum.

Amidst it all—the wild seas, the unknown stars, the tattooed peoples strange—did Franklin keep the locket close and his longing closer still.

There came a starlit night upon the Swan's foredeck when Agèd Albert said: "Well I perceive, me lad, thy heart's not in our chanteys, jigs or drinking songs, lusty though they be. Nor is thy noble mind attuned to the daily duty of thy hands and back. Among the happy folks of these most happy isles, me lad, find thee a maiden here, and spare us all thy fret and this, thy vacant gaze."

"I hear thy plain concerns and harken I do," said young Franklin back. "Yet, ne'er shall my heart leave fair Constance 'lorn, for she's my guiding star!"

Then, a calm befell the Silver Swan and all her crew, the like of which they'd ne'er known. The seas grew hushed and smooth as glass. The sun, an angry god that burned the decks day by day, 'til the tar that held her tight did drip from the ship's brave hull.

First, up dried the rum. Then turned the kegs of water green. And then, the mariners dropped down one by one; and with a weary groan, the Silver Swan herself went down.

Of them all, there survived but two: Agèd Albert and young Franklin did cling onto a spar and floated 'neath the cloudless sky upon a nameless sea.

"Of all have we alone survived and may survive to tell," now moaned the bones that Agèd Albert were.

"'Tis true; yet must I somehow find my home and greet my Constance dear, and dry her tears and touch her cheek and speak her name once more," the skeleton that Franklin was did groan.

These two lost sailors did at last drift up onto an isle that was so small in half a day thou could around it pace; and there upon they dwelt for many a tedious year. Wild as tares their beards did grow; more ragged than a beggar's, their seamen's weeds did hang; and their very words did shrink to grunts of "aye" or "nay"—for what else was there left to them to say?

Then came a day like every other on that small isle when there appeared a sail. Anon, a majestic frigate drew nigh, and hale faces in wonder peered at the wild beasts waving and moaning upon its sandy shore.

"At last my Constance shall I see once more," thought seaman Franklin then, and tears of salt rained from his sun-bleared eyes.

"At last shall I taste rum again," thought Agèd Albert, and salty tears from his blear eyes did pour out like rain.

'Twas all of twenty years since the Silver Swan went down. The sailors' wives, their sweethearts dear and betrothèds, one by one, the bitter pill had swallowed and taken someone new. The gallant crew, they monumented upon the village green; and, for a time, did place nosegays to grace it every day.

But those bright blooms did less appear...and then, none appeared at all—save for the lone red rose that pledged Constance's love for her lost Franklin brave.

Nor was Time more kind on land than 'twas at sea. Too soon, her golden tresses dulled, her crystal eyes grew cloudy. The string of patient days upon her weighed, 'til, like a waning moon, she bent into a crescent shape. And now, she seemed a spinster eld, like them that dwell at hamlet's edge in silence, like a nun.

'Twas long ago that village wives had urged she stow her grief and take another man of sea or land. To them had Constance this to say: "'Tis Fidelity, not Grief, that rules my heart, and when my Franklin shall return, how bright shall shine his brow! How glad my heart shall sing!"

Long did the proud frigate wander with gaunt Franklin, and Agèd Albert, too, aboard. So long it was, in truth, that Albert found his flood of speech once more and told poor Franklin this:

"Deep have I pondered and hard, me lad, and I resolve

to ride this vessel proud to Portsmouth, thence to London fair. For, all these years gone by, none in our village remains who'll love or care 'bout me.

"But certain sure am I that I shall find some poet poor or piebald balladeer that of my tales will rhyme. Then shall London town—I doubt it not—echo the tale of so ancient a mariner as I, and shalt a life of fame and fortune and buxom wenches three be mine. 'Tis but the work of days, I ween, to find so crafty a one."

To which good Franklin did reply: "I wish thee luck, old mariner; for thou hast been these twenty years, a boon companion true. Yet, I be bound where Constance waits, and where her love still shineth bright."

"Why, bless thee, then, my simple swain," the ancient mariner said. "Would that it haps as thou dost dream—though I do doubt the world shall brook a wonder such as thine."

To London, then, did Albert go; whilst Franklin crossed both wood and field, town and hamlet 'til he stepped at last, twenty-one years less but a day, upon his village green.

There, 'neath the pale-faced moon, he traced his name among those lost when the Silver Swan went down. And there spied he a single rose astride the mossy stones.

Then sits him down, and tears do wet his leath'ry cheeks. For, whilst he lived, hope did live too. But now, what love could'st still there be for one so longtime dead as he?

Comes first light, and a figure nears, arced like a waning moon. Up starts a shape, more bones than man, and halts the old moon in her course. For an instant there did nothing stir in stars above or waters deep.

Then fly those two, each to the other—and, who dares tell how sweet their embrace would be?

The World and Time do grievous tolls exact—save in our loving eyes. For there live on remembered smiles and rosy cheeks and noble brows untouched by Fact, unmarred by Fate.

Had any drowsy 'prentice boy then crept upon our green, how rare a sight his eyes would greet: a skeleton and crescent moon waltzing arm in arm!

Tale the Eighth
Glorianna, the Goat-girl

Where once the village ended and the pastures and wolds began, nestled the cottage of James the Shepherd and his goodwife, Mathilda. There they dwelt with the daughter they loved above all else, Glorianna, the one they called *Morning Glory*—for such was the joy she did bring them each new day.

Morning Glory gazed upon the fragrant pastures, the shadowy wood and the wide, blue welkin through wondering emerald eyes. Sleek as a raven's wing her tresses grew; and she loved naught more than to roam hill and vale the day long, watching o'er her father's flock. In this manner did Morning Glory grow, fleet as the wind and blithe as song; and yet, of town or hamlet as innocent as any suckling lamb.

"I sorely fear the day," sighed James oft, "when the village swains come a-courting, as a-courting they'll surely come. Nor know I how our dear Morning Glory may veil herself from this world wide and its many evils."

"Aye, 'tis so," agreed Mathilda. "Yet, our darling girl must needs 'front the world and what it holds, for she'll not be a child much longer. In sooth, we should do something to forewarn her."

Thus did the doting wife and the o'er fond husband shilly-shally well past the day Morning Glory crossed o'er the threshold of maidenhood.

Now, it so hapt that in the village there dwelt three foul men, whose useful days long since had flown—if e'er useful days there had been. Noxious Nathan, Leering Lawrence, and Awful Erwin were they named, and many a tedious hour they lolled about the village green near the Monument to Our Forgotten Sailors.

Lank and sallow was Leering Lawrence; Erwin was stout and dun as a paving stone; whilst from atop Nathan's head sprouted a few rust hairs like lone stalks in last winter's field. From the chin of each dangled grey beards slicked with porridge and ale.

Not widow, nor wife, nor maid, nor spinster could pass them by without whoops or whistles from these odious three.

"Be thee lonely, my lovely? Well can I scratch that itch for you," would Erwin offer.

"I've something here in my pocket thou must surely be a-longing for," Nathan would proffer.

The while, his mouth agape with sooty teeth, would Lawrence's ruddy eyes devour each lass or lady as a ravenous wolf looks o'er a flock of shuddering ewes.

Nor were the Village Elders apt to restrain these three, despite their women's many complaints. For, whene'er the Elders 'fronted the three vile layabouts, thus would go the debate:

First would Nathan aver, "Alas, 'tis naught of our choosing nor within our control. 'Tis but the way both God and Nature hath shaped us."

"The day since Father Adam laid eyes upon his buxom Eve, 'twas e'er thus," would Erwin reason further. "As well might ye essay to alter wind, flood or fire as change how man and woman be made."

"Besides, 'tis but harmless fun. What if lass or lady taketh it ill? She'll get o'er it right soon enow. Considered proper, 'tis more of a compliment to 'er fer bein' so allurin'," would Nathan grandly conclude.

At this would the Elders shrug their narrow shoulders, scratch their greying skulls, and repair in defeat to the Swan and Duck.

Anon, it came to pass that the three old idlers learned—to this day no one will say how—that Morning Glory was soon to be a woman, and fain would they look upon her. Out crept they from the village that very eve unto the gladèd pool wherein Morning Glory did wash herself of the day's heat and dust. There crouched these greybeards among the reeds and grasses that stand thick and tall beside those crystalline waters.

Thence came beauteous Morning Glory. Casting aside her shepherd's weeds, into the pool she waded, and, with a sweet song of pasture and fresh wood, 'gan to bathe therein.

"Hail, lovely *Mädchen*," rasped out a voice. "Have I a little surprise for you!"

"Nay, have I a better 'un—and 'tis a bigger 'un, too!" said another.

"Let me come and warsh your pretty back," said the first voice.

"Let me but scrub those dainty hips and thighs. You'll like it well enow, I ween, when all's been done and said," added the second voice.

"And be left a-wantin' for more, I wager," rasped out the first.

Young Morning Glory understood at what the foul voices hinted but dimly, yet well did she perceive their vile intent. Then, she spied a pair of red-rimmed eyes leering from amidst the reeds; and of a sudden, the waters around her grew dark and chill and cold.

Thereafter did three greasy figures appear, like gnats upon ripe windfall, ogling and a-calling after young Morning Glory. Nor could she escape their crude voices in her mind, for there, too, did their coarse caws echo.

Then James and Mathilda perceived a change come over their dear child as though a wintry cloud had passed twixt earth and April sun. Deep furrows crossed her clear brow; haunted were her emerald eyes, and silent went her sweet songs of wood and heath.

Not a word did Morning Glory speak of that which vexed her sore. Nor ventured she forth with their goats and sheep, e'en though the days were fair and the pastures melodious with songs of the lark. No; sat she still, shamed and confused, beside their lowly hearth, gazing at her feet.

"We must discover what weighs so upon our Morning Glory," urged James. "Let us send at once for the old woman what lives deep within the forest. Wise she is in mysteries of the heart, be it young or be it eld. Surely she shall aid us."

Ebon were the old woman's robes that day and somber were her eyes as she leaned upon her stick of yew and studied the sullen lass hunched by the humble hearth. After a time, she spoke gently and privily to the girl. Long did they talk, heads close together, 'til well past the fire's dying and the setting of the moon.

At first light, up sprang fair Morning Glory, kissed her mother and father *adieu*, and announced she was off to tend their flocks.

"All is now repaired," said the agèd one. "And all will be well with thy dear daughter—albeit of some others, I durst not say the same." With these dark words, she did leave the good shepherd and his wife.

Then James spied three bearded billy goats in his goat pen, the likes of which he'd not seen at evensong. One was long and lank with reddened eyes; the second round and of a dusky hue; and the third had but sparse rust hairs atop its knobby head.

There stood this sad trio, bleating like sackbuts the day long at the nannies in the pasture beyond...who wisely paid them no heed. Nor durst James loose them amidst his flock, for they were of uncertain origin and exceedingly foul of breath.

"'Tis a mystery," quoth James, gazing in puzzlement upon the three penned goats.

"'Tis a miracle," said Mathilda; "though, to be sure, 'tis an oddish one."

"'Tis mostly a relief," whispered Morning Glory, as she led the ewes forth unto her father's pastures with a lightsome step and knowing smile.

Tale the Ninth
The Mountain of Gold

Once there was a realm ruled by King Walter the Kind and Queen Wilma the Beneficent. For two score years and more they did helm their kingdom toward prosperity and peace.

Its market square did hum with trade, as burgher and farmer, peasant and squire got and spent 'neath colored awnings, in the shops and the alleyways. And all 'round, the cheerful peal of gold and silver coin upon coin did chime.

Among this happy, prosperous throng dwelt the Margrave Mountgeld, a noble of ancient line, who owned both forest and field as far as eye could see. Rich indeed he was, endowed for his life and more with all the Flemish wine, German beef, and spices from the Indies he, or any other, could e'er desire.

And yet, this rich margrave was ill at ease. For, he was cursed inward by that great archenemy of Content: Ambition.

"Well-a-day," sighed this margrave, "what hath a man to live for—be he base or royal—when he possesseth already all that his heart may desire? Comfort and plenty have I known since my natal hour, and in such dull condition 'tis like I shall die."

Mooning thus one day, his eye fell upon a pile of golden gilders, the which his ragged tenants had heaped within his counting house in discharge of their steep rents.

"These gilders make a beauteous sight," mused the margrave. "Fairer than the fairest maid. More bright than the stars or sun in the sky. More blessèd to mine ear is their ring than a year of evensongs.

"Why now, here's a thought aborning: why should I not strive to gather about me all the gold and silver there be in this realm and heap it up here in my counting house? 'Twill be a triumph that shall make me the envy and talk of all the court and all the country hereabout."

Then did Margrave Mountgeld ingeniously set about grasping each and every coin e'er minted in King Walter and Queen Wilma's realm. He sold his lands for cash on the barrelhead. He sold his kine, he sold his flocks. He sold his furnishings and his silks, his tapestries and fine embroidered tablecloths. Sold he his family's portraits down from the walls, their gleaming suits of armor, their swords and pikes from the great hall.

'Twas said that the Margrave Mountgeld would sell the very sun and moon to the highest bidder, could he but find such a one. All the while, the gold and silver mountain in his counting house grew wider and higher still.

Yet, it grew not fast nor high enough for him, for did he not hear the ring of coin on coin still echoing from market stall and shop e'en to the empty chambers of Mountgeld Hall?

"This fadgeth not," stewed the margrave. "So long as the king's treasury holds gold, I shall never have it all. Alas, my great enterprise is doomed, and I to fail."

By strange chance then the margrave's steely eye lit upon an ancient lamp of bass heaped carelessly there amidst his silver and gold hoard.

"Odd," thought he. "Ne'er have I seen that afore. I ween that, with but a little spit and polish, it may fetch me a copper shekel or two." And, with his sole remaining silk handkerchief, he set about rubbing the old vessel.

In an instant, the counting house filled with azure smoke and appeared therein a bronzed man in a yellow silk turban bright as the sun and ample scarlet pantaloons.

"Hold! Who be ye!" exclaimed the margrave. Fain would he have called his guards, but had he dismissed them one and all to save their keep.

"To some I be Dennis the Djinn," replied the figure. "But thou may call me Gene. Zounds, how I do love that grand entrance! 'Tis better than the opera, dost thou not think?" Then did Dennis—or Gene—stretch his powerful arms above his head and yawn. "Goodness me, what a sleep I've had!"

"What art thou doing in my counting house?" demanded the margrave.

"Restrain thy horses, brother, and do but recall 'twas thee who summoned me. Pray, what be the nature of thy problem? Truth to tell, this seems a rather drab and empty mansion, and there be places I'd much rather be."

To this replied the margrave naught, though his eyes grew rounder and his mouth gaped wider.

"Speechless art thou? Tut, I oft have that effect on people," said the djinn. "I'll explain: thy wish is my command. Some, for example, wish for happiness; others for love (the two be ne'er the same, as it falls out).

"Still others desire unbounded power, and a few want to live on for e'er and a day (also, a big mistake in my view—take it from one who's tried). Whate'er they do ask, that do I grant without further ado. Now then, what be thy fondest desire?"

From within his fog, the margrave blurted out: "To possess all the gold and silver in the kingdom, down to the very last copper, and heap it up here in my counting house."

"You've pondered on this, I ween," said Dennis—or rather, Gene.

"Aye," said the Margrave Mountgeld. "Not love, nor life, nor power, but all this realm's gold is my heart's desire."

"So shalt thou have it, then," said this imp o' the lamp. And he vanished into the cloud of azure smoke, which did flow back into the lamp as water whirls out through a hole in a leathern bucket.

The next morning but two, the Lord Chamberlain appeared before King Walter and Queen Wilma, e'en as they breakfasted on their kippers and pungent cheese.

"My Lord," quoth the Lord Chamberlain, "I bring sad tidings from the treasury. It appeareth that nor golden gilder nor silver crown remains. Some way, all have vanished."

"Hmm," mused King Walter. "May we not mint more

gilders and crowns of gold?"

"Alas, my Lord," replied the wise, old Chamberlain. "When did we so in '56, the worth of the gilder dropped like an arrowed pheasant from the sky. And more: there remain no gold bars within the King's Treasury from which to mint."

"Indeed?" spoke up the e'er practical Queen Wilma. "'Tis a situation without precedent then. Let us lay it before the Royal Council. 'Tis what we feed and robe and house 'em for, after all."

Within the hour was the Royal Council seated within its chambers, waited upon by knights and ladies and their pages and ladies-in-waiting. Ripe fruits and delicate viands were set before them, but none dared partake, for well they perceived, should no remedies be found, an army of ills marching towards their kingdom like a storm rolling in o'er the distant hills.

"Already, Sire," reported Duke Rodney, "the simple people be alarmed. And, silent and still as death be the market stalls, shops and alleyways. Without gilders or crowns, there's no happy sounds of commerce."

"Alas," "Ah, me," "Oh, woe," and "Heavens above," chimed in the Council. Yet, nary an idea sprang forth from grey heads or tumbled forth from grey beards.

Then, up spoke the young page Alan from his station by the chamber door: "My good lords and ladies," quoth he. "Well am I aware that I be but a babe among wise men and but a mere page among my betters. Yet harken, prithee, to what I say...

"When I was but a lad, happily at play along the riverbank, oft would we gather the black and white river stones to use in our games of barter. All agreed that a white stone was the equal of five black stones and that a black stone could purchase a small loaf. Then, played we at buying and selling until the kine came home, as blithe in our childish game as though were we kings. For, in fine, what is gold or silver but a toy that we agree, both one and all, to hold dear?"

Not long did King Walter the Kind ponder over Alan's impertinence afore he sprung—as much as an agèd man can spring—into Regal Action. Out from the castle issued his Knights Errant to the river, wherefrom they collected a marvelous hoard of white and black stones from the bed and bank.

Forth into every village and town then issued the king's ministers, with hastily penned proclamations. By the next day but one, there appeared in every market square a cart of river stones and a Minister of the Treasury, who meted them out justly among the people.

Nor was it long thereafter but the markets did resume their busy trade, as bread and milk and cheese and honey and fine cloth and wooden clogs and iron implements and artfully decorated icons and metal pots and joints of beef exchanged hands to the rhythmic music, not of gold and silver, but of stone upon stone.

Thus, the old kingdom of King Walter the Kind and Queen Wilma the Beneficent did prosper once again.

Came then the puffed-up Margrave Mountgeld into the town, wherein he witnessed all these transactions and more.

"How be they still getting and spending? Have I not harvested all the golden gilders and silver crowns and what-hath-thous in the realm?" he fumed. "Why art they not gazing with envy on me and my mountain of gold?"

At this very moment, there hastened by a stooped old woman bearing her load of hay to market.

"Thou there, thou peasant," hailed the margrave. "Here will I give thee three golden gilders and a silver shilling for that load thou bearest. What sayest thou? Bargain?"

"Why, my good lord; of what use be thy gilders and shillings to me? As no others in the market desire them, well might they be wisps of smoke or idle dreams, of so little worth they are.

"That aside, have I not stones enow, both black and white, hidden away here and there within my tattered weeds, to buy me bread and drink sufficient to the day?" And on paced this peasant woman to market.

Thence, to his hollow keep, the margrave retired with painful steps and slow. Lovingly he cast mournful eyes over the glittering mountain of gold there amassed; and to the top of that gleaming heap he climbed.

"As well might I sit here as on a remote isle for all the good this hoard doeth me," mused the margrave. "For, all that I have gained amounts but to a hill of beans if no one else covets it."

And there, to this very day, glumly perches the Margrave Mountgeld, like frosty snow atop a forlorn scarp. There he sighs his wintry sighs, whilst through his fingers the bright coins do sift and tumble like sands within an hourglass.

Ṭale the Ṭenth
The Ēnmity of Ṭish for Ṭosh and Ṭosh for Ṭish

Long rang the cheers and echoed loud the huzzahs when the Grand Vizier sent out word that His Exalted Highness, the Most Regal of Sultans, had again become a father—not merely once, but twice o'er. For, though the Princess Salomay was much belovèd in every corner of her father's caliphate, such were the customs of that land and that time that those governed did prefer their governors to be male.

Within the palace walls, howe'er, the birth of the princeling twins, Tish and Tosh, brought joy alloyed with worry. Troubled and restless had they been within the womb of the First Wife of the great Sultan. And, when the twins entered this world, they entered locked in enmity. At the very moment of birth was Tish's tiny fist thrust hard into Tosh's tiny eye and Tosh's small foot kicking sharp against Tish's wee shin.

"'Tis but the result of so much time in so cramped a space," announced the midwife to the anxious mother and her husband. "Get o'er it anon, they will." At which, in haste, she gathered up her golden drachma and scurried off.

In no time, the midwife's assurances did prove mistaken. Tish and Tosh were ever at one another's throats, morn and eve; and, as they grew, their battles grew as well. There were bumps and scrapes, bruises, cuts and scratches, and arguments enow to fill the great library at Alexandria.

"Tosh took my silk sash," raged Tish as he struck at his brother.

"Tish is seated on my very own hassock of gold," howled Tosh, slashing at his brother.

Each eve at bedtime, the princelings' weary nurses would stagger home to their families and their beds, as bruised and bloodied as foot soldiers home from mortal combat.

The older the princelings grew, the more lethal did their conflicts become. Once, Tosh discovered a venomous viper lurking in a silver bowl of fresh apricots. On an evening, Tish threw back the silken sheets of his bed to find an angry scorpion lurking therein. A rusted nail found its way through the sole of Tosh's blue slipper; a braid of sharp thorns nestled in the crown of Tish's silk turban.

No sooner were the princes introduced to the arts of the scimitar and dirk, then scratches and bruises turned to wounds that took the most skilled of the caliphate's physicians to plaster o'er.

At last did the weary Sultan, his Grand Vizier, and the head Imam summon the two princes before them.

"What ails thee?" demanded the Sultan, their father. "Whence cometh this ceaseless conflict betwixt and between ye two? Do I not provide each of thee with all thy heart's desires?"

"Aye, added the Imam, his long, grey beard atremble; "and have ye not ta'en to heart the sacred verses that I have taught ye abjuring us all to love our brothers as we do ourselves?"

The two young men stood silent for a moment. Then up spoke Prince Tish, the while menacing his brother with a right fist recently minus two fingers:

"I cannot say the cause, dear Father. Thus it hath been for as long as my wits recall. Yet, I cannot bear to breathe the selfsame air this vile person breathes, for his very exhalations offend me to my core."

Prince Tosh glared at his brother with his one remaining eye: "Nay, beloved Sire, this creature offends me so deeply that, were I to tread the same path that he hath trod but one time, 'twould be as if a thousand daggers were thrust into the soles of my feet. I know not why, but 'tis most avowedly so."

"This caliphate and all the desert round 'tis not big enough to contain the both of us," rejoined Prince Tish haughtily.

"Nor can I be at peace in a world that tolerates so toadsome a creature as this," said Prince Tosh, with his one eye blazing like fire.

Seeing his sons thus hard and unmoving as two stones, the sorrowful Sultan exiled the brothers to the furthest corners of his caliphate. Alas, 'twas not long after that each brother raised up an army in his satrap, fed daily on hatred of the Tishers or the Toshers. Thence did skirmishes and raids originate, both night and day, until the people in the middle provinces were both war-weary and terrified.

"Great and most potent One," intoned the Grand Vizier then. "Oh, most wonderful Sultan of Sultans, I fear something must be done, and quickly. Thy lands be falling into tatters under the onslaught of this bitter and senseless feud. Nor see I an end to this woeful chaos and bloodletting."

"As 'tis so, I fear I must now do as my father and his father before him hath done," sighed the Sultan of Sultans; and, from beneath a silken cushion of his royal throne, he tugged out an ancient oil lamp of brass.

No sooner had the somber Sultan rubbed his hand upon the lamp than the throne room was filled with azure smoke. From within the billows of which stepped forth a djinn, robed in scarlet pantaloons and a jeweled turban, yellow as the sun above.

"Praise Allah," exclaimed this djinn. "Oh, how I love that grand entrance! Is it not better than a fanfare of trumpets or train of dancing maidens, or e'en a troupe of elephants, trunks grasping tails?"

"My father hath warned me about thee," said the Sultan of Sultans warily. "Thou art as full of tricks as an otter and yet, also, most powerful and wise."

"'Tis interesting to see it that way," replied the djinn. "For, I too have my bounds and limits to observe, as even doth thou. And there be strict rules, too, I must obey. Nor can I alter the hearts of men—much as they may need my improving. For that power, I would have to petition—in triplicate, mind thou—and that tedium am I loathe to undertake. Natheless, things being what they be, what may I do for thee, Eminence?"

The Sultan, assisted by his Grand Vizier and the sputtering Imam, detailed their sad dilemma. The djinn looked bored and pared his nails during their long-winded and woe-laden tale of Prince Tish and Prince Tosh's relentless enmity.

"'Tis unfortunate ye have waited this long," said the djinn at last, casually dusting a mote off his silk pantaloons. "Far too oft do those in power wink at such discords. Hatred is a bitter plant that, once allowed to root, is all but impossible to remove. But, such is the world ye live in, and there's little use in shedding tears o'er honey'd tea already spilt. List ye; here is what ye must do to restore peace unto your kingdom . . ."

Heaving a great sigh, the strife-weary Sultan and his sage advisors did then agree to the djinn's plan.

A week and a day thereafter, two ignorant armies faced one another across a dusty plain as the weary sun rose o'er the desert. High and proud fluttered the red silk banners of the Army of Prince Tish, and brightly did the sun seem to burn from their burnished swords and shields. Proud and high furled the gold silk banners of the Army of Prince Tosh, and the sun's rays that glinted from their spears and shields pierced the eyes of onlookers like shards of glass.

Each force screamed curses at the other: they insulted one another's mothers; they threatened one another's sisters; they vowed to steal one another's sheep and to make off with one another's camels, and ne'er to rest until the other was ground into the dust beneath their sandals. Each called the other ugly and claimed they laced their mutton stews with the dung of dogs.

On the top of a small mountain nearby, where reposed the Sultan of Sultans and his retinue on cushions of silk and satin, up started a figure in a bright turban and the reddest of pantaloons. Raising the Royal Ram's Horn to his lips, this figure blew a long and mournful blast.

At this signal, the opposing armies flooded forth with screams like banshees, each led by Prince Tish or Prince Tosh. Like the desert wind, so rushed these two brothers across the dusty plain, outstripping their followers in their eager wrath.

The two princes came together with so violent a force that their two armies stood stock still in awe, watching the twins writhe, twist, swirl, snarl and spin in a fierce dance of mutual loathing.

Prince Tosh held Prince Tish by his long, dark braid and would have slit his throat but that Prince Tish had his knee in Prince Tosh's groin and his thumb in Tosh's one remaining eye. Faster and faster spun the two brothers 'round until the onlookers could no longer tell the one from the other.

As they spun and swirled thus, up rose the dust of the plain around their ankles, thence to their waists, and then to their shoulders and heads. Anon, all that the Sultan of Sultans, the two great armies, and the royal retinue could see was a whirling cloud of dust that twisted and spun like a child's top. And then, it danced and swirled its way across the dusty plain and over a far dune, where it vanished from sight.

"Thus were they e'en in the womb," observed the First Wife of the Sultan, "ever a-tumbling and a-twisting like an August monsoon 'til methought I should burst."

"And thus will they be 'til meet they their destined ends, I shouldn't wonder," said the Sultan of Sultans, with a tear in his grey eye. "The Princess Salomay shalt rule our realm in their stead when we are gone, and long may she govern a people that have learned the value of tolerance, if not peace."

And, in time, it came to pass.

Long and well did Salomay reign o'er this ancient caliphate; and should one under her beneficent rule fall out with another, why, had she not but to nod toward the whirling dust devils of the desert and the parties would hastily put down their swords and lay aside their dispute and embrace one another as true brothers ought?

Tale the Eleventh
The Perfect Princess

Not so very long ago, in a kingdom not so very far away, reigned earnest King Robert the Redear and his good Queen Hilda. Now, King Robert and Queen Hilda were the very sort of queen and king any subject could wish for, for they were both good and determined to be even better.

"My beloved queen," King Robert did oft observe at night in the Royal Bedchambers, "sooth is that we must strive our utmost, for 'tis my heart's ambition to win renown as the best king e'er there was."

"Aye," agreed good Queen Hilda; "and 'tis my long-simmering desire to be remembered the wide-realm o'er as the best queen and helpmate e'er there was."

In such harmonious ambition did the regal couple sink into their royal slumbers on that and every night.

As Royal Ambition dictated, Queen Hilda and King Robert resolved to make their palace and all within it the very model of a modern monarchy. They filled the Royal Library with the latest tomes from Paris and Milan and with gilt-edged volumes penned by the worthiest ancients of Persia, Greece and Alexandria.

The Great Hall and Royal Sitting Rooms gleamed with the torsos of Greek and Roman gods carved in the whitest marble from the hills of Carrara. The Royal Place Settings were of silver forged in the hellish fires of Hammersmith; and the Royal Cupboard teamed with the most delicate and pure leaded crystal from Bavaria. Magnificent tapestries from Flanders hung in their halls, where the ceilings were adorned with pastoral scenes of all four seasons through the magical ministrations of Italian mural masters.

Into the Royal Fountain in the Royal Courtyard gushed frothy torrents from the mouths of lions and dolphins by means of an ingenious mechanism only just devised in France; and the Royal Barge that bobbed upon the Royal Lake was nothing other than an East Indian dhow.

"Have we not created the very best castle and court there e'er could be?" reasoned Queen Hilda. "Is our crystal not all but invisible to hand and our fine silver the most substantial? After all 'tis done and said, what boots it were we to attain but a middling prize?"

"Right as ever, my good queen," replied King Robert. "Yet, to be the best of rulers, must we not also embody each and every noble aspiration *sans* rest, lest our people fall into slough-eyed content and our precious kingdom falter in its high promise?"

Reasoning thus, the driven king and queen did lead

forth the lords and ladies, dukes and duchesses, burghers and burghers' wives, yeomen and peasants in a restless pavane of *'tis good—but not yet good enough.*

It so happed that King Robert and Queen Hilda had but one child, though they did toil, oft and mightily, to procure a second. A lovely princess was she, with eyes of a summer sky at twilight and hair bright as copper. E'er at the princess's right hand stood Humphrey, her Royal Tutor, and, but a pace or two behind, hover'd Howard, her faithful page.

"Prithee tell us, good Humphrey, how goeth the princess's instruction?" inquired the queen and king each evening. "For, well thou knowest 'tis our Regal Desire that she become the best-belovèd princess—and queen thereafter—the world hast ever known. We are counting on you to bring her toes to the mark."

"Well, well and well," replied the Royal Tutor in haste. "The princess is a remarkable quick study and a swift and sure mistress of all she undertaketh."

True enow were the tutor's words, for he and the faithful Howard did drill her mercilessly each and every day in all the arts appertaining to a young monarch.

Humphrey taught the little princess to ride the powerful grey gelding, Astrolix, like thistle down before the wind, whilst young Howard jolted along in his saddle behind. Humphrey drilled the princess in the intricate steps of minuet and *haute* dancing, 'til weary Howard's legs could bear him up no longer.

The Royal Tutor schooled the princess in both the long- and the cross-bow until, with hands no longer trembling, she could draw upon and split a pippin perched atop Howard's quivering pate. Drilled she too in the handling of epée, mace and lance, all in the ill event that she become a spinster queen, 'till bruisèd Howard cried "Hold; enough! I must rest and staunch my flowing wounds, lest upon the princess's silk robes I bleed."

Then Humphrey sat the princess down afore a banquet fit for a king and drilled her in the purpose and utility of each and all the fine silver spoons and knives and goblets of clearest Bavarian crystal. Nor was her long day then o'er, for there was Latin to master, and the geography of the realms all about to learn, and the chart of the heavens to memorize, and the names, titles and descendants of her ancestors innumerable to recite.

Then also did she sit in mock judgment over the disputes of her subjects. Such as when the yeomen, Carleton and Stefan, did each stoutly swear that a wee black lamb was his own and no other's. Long did the princess attend to their tiresome plaints and cross-accusations, until her eyelids grew heavy and spent Howard fell a-snoring behind her little throne.

"Seeing as how neither of thee will yield, yet both be immovable as stones in a pasture wall, so I decree that ye slay the lamb forthwith and divide its meat and bones and blood equally betwixt ye," declared the princess at last, as sage Humphrey nodded his approval.

Thus hard and at great pains the princess toiled. Yet e'en as her skill and mastery increased, so grew she more pale and wan.

"Thou must needs get more fresh air," observed King Robert one morning over his Royal Kippers and Toasts.

"Aye," said Queen Hilda. "The ideal monarch must always body forth the very picture of rosy health."

"Mayhap I need not be ideal," muttered the princess

softly. "Mayhap I may be but myself, as I am."

"What sayeth thou?" asked Queen Hilda sharply.

"What canst thou mean?" blustered King Robert with alarm. "Why, have not we and good Humphrey here devoted every waking moment—and a good many dreary watches—to sculpting thee into the very form and substance of the perfect princess? Shalt thou not be as clear and bright as the crystal glass that bears thy Rhenish wine? 'Tis thy destiny, my child; 'tis the glory to which thou wert born."

"And though mightily do we hunger for thy success, darling girl, 'tis for thee and thee alone this be done, so that all will love and admire thee even more than they now do us," added the queen, as Humphrey nodded with deep gravity and poor Howard gazed at the ceiling.

"As you wish, dear mother and father," replied the princess, looking yet paler still.

So did the princess's daily round of jousting and riding, Latin and royal etiquette, fencing and dancing and petty petitions continue apace. To which Humphrey and loyal Howard added a morning dash o'er field and down in hopes of deepening thereby the roseate hue of the princess's cheek whilst improving her endurance also.

So did the insistent care of King Robert and Queen Hilda fill the girl's every day and watchful night.

"Thou art doing excellent well, my darling dear," said earnest King Robert. "Keep up the good labor!"

"'Tis but a few strides more to the finish, my angel," cheered on good Queen Hilda; "whereat thou shalt make us all very, very proud."

"Thou best eat more flesh to beef up thy strength," interjected the Royal Tutor Humphrey, and summoned he a serving man bearing a steaming platter of venison liver. This the princess did dutifully nibble upon, saying to herself alone, "Would that I might be just she who I am."

All this while did watchful Howard observe the princess fade, as doth the moon at first daylight, and grow more lucent, as do the petals of a rose when long pressed within a musty psalter.

'Twas not long hereafter that the king, queen and Royal Tutor put their heads together in private concourse.

"What say ye, Humphrey? Doth our princess be well versed in each and every art that becometh a monarch? Is she not as pure and as refined as 'tis possible she be?"

"Sire, she hath mastered all and more than I can teach her—and that be a goodly amount, if I may be so bold," replied Humphrey with pride. "Ready she is for the adulation of her people. I say let us parade her forth forthwith."

"The perfect princess," said Queen Hilda; "is our great and ultimate work of statecraft, my good husband. Let the *hosannas* ring and praises be sung for this, our capstone achievement."

"Aye," said the proud king. "She has turned out e'en better than we dared hope . . . and some small credit goeth to thee, my dear Humphrey. The princess is perfect, that be crystal clear."

The next day but one, silken banners fluttered from the palace battlements and bright ribbons of gold and blue adorned the trees and way posts along the roads unto the hamlet square. At noon precisely did twelve brass trumpets sound and the palace gates swing wide to let the Royal Procession wend its glittering way forth.

King Robert the Redear and Queen Hilda led this regal

troupe, robed in the finest velvet and ermine. Behind them strolled the Royal Tutor Humphrey, wrapped about in his scholastic robes, hood and university cap. He was flanked round and about by knights and their ladies fitted out in raiment the colors of the rainbow.

"Where be the princess?" whispered a peasant standing by. "Which one be she?"

"I perceive her not," replied his wife, "only the refined lords and ladies of the court."

"Were we not instructed to behold the Perfection of all Perfections?" whispered the husband. "Is not our princess the very apex of the queen and king's desires and the fruit of their long, loving labors?"

"Listen to thee go on then," sneered the peasant's wife. "'Apex' is it? See her I do not—only a gap there amidst the royal parade wherein she may walk, were she a mind to."

A pace or two behind the royal procession trudged the ever loyal Page Howard. Fixed was his mournful gaze upon the empty space behind the proud king and queen. There, the little princess did obediently walk, refined and purified and well nigh invisible, her head bowed and her eyes cast down as though she were a pious novitiate.

Faithful Howard—and he alone it seemed—was yet able to trace the faintest lineaments of this perfect, crystal princess.

Tale the Twelfth
The Clever Tailor

Once upon a dark eve, Derwent the Tailor sat cross-legged upon the dusty floor of his mean shop, sewing Belgian brocade onto a fine lady's wedding gown. Long had Derwent labored there, down the narrow alley behind the Swan and Duck, stitching the finery of lords and ladies and the well-worn weeds, as well, of yeomen and waiting maids.

In truth, the little tailor had so long sewn and stitched, darned and tatted, that his ancient fingers worked now mostly of their own accord, whilst their master's mind roved 'midst loves and laughter long since past.

There again Derwent saw the blooming cheeks of the maid he'd wooed and lost to that rogue and wild tinker. In his mind's ear echoed the boyish shouts of the brother whose young life had ended 'ere it began; and there again felt he the soft caress of she who had, many years since, trod the narrow, shaded path of shadows.

So worked his fingers, dropping nary a stitch, and so roved his mind, both far and wide.

In that dim gloaming on that dusky eve, there appeared of a sudden a hooded figure in the little tailor's doorway. "Be thou Derwent the tailor?" quoth the gaunt stranger.

"So be I he," replied Derwent, laying aside his tedious task. "Pray sir, bend low thy exalted head and enter."

Low bent the grim visitor and passed beneath Derwent's rough-hewn lintel.

"Prithee sir, lay aside that ebon crook thou carries and tell me what I may do for thee," said the little tailor.

"'Tis naught what thou canst do for me that brings me hence," replied his gloomy guest. "'Tis what I've come to do to thee."

Then a light gleamed deep within the wily tailor's eyes as up he spake: "And thou hast come to the place proper, I assure thee, for well I perceive thou art in need of my skills."

"I fear thou misapprehend," objected the somber stranger.

"Nay, sir; for all about thee is the aura of weariness and sore fatigue. Your ceaseless labors weigh heavily upon thee, I ween, and fain wouldst thou rest a while. Why, look thou, sir, how dusty and drear thy raiment be. Surely, such rags alone would make many a man weary."

"'Tis true enough," sighed the glum guest. "Indeed, there be so many more of ye these latter days than e'er before. But come. I canna tarry here long."

"'Twill be but a twinkling and a trice, sir. For the

nonce, sit thee down upon yon bail of worsted wool and I shall fetch us tea and oat cakes. And pray, do lay aside that fearsome crook thou wieldeth."

With a sigh like a January wind, the stranger did as he was bid, and the little tailor bustled about in the dim recess of his shop.

"Here now: tea and cake and rest for thy weary bones (for thou art a bony one in sooth)," said Derwent anon.

"Much hast thou traveled the wild world in that ancient cloak of thine, I surmise," Derwent went on. "Now 'tis frayed, worn and stained. Nor do its folds hang at all gracefully upon thy lean and lanky frame. Indeed, I am somewhat surprised that one of thy standing is able to prosecute his business in a cloak of so little dignity. Have I not seen a mere shepherd's boy more suitably attired?"

Then gazed the stranger at the sleeve of his dusky garb, taking its frayed cuff 'twixt a boney thumb and forefinger. "'Tis true enow," mused he after a moment's thought. "Little heed have I paid to my dress these days. Not that I'm in the market for costly garments," he added hastily.

"No, sir; not at all," rejoined the bland tailor. "For I can see thou art well-schooled in the ways of the world and appreciate the value of a farthing."

"As 'tis saved, 'tis earned," murmured the gloomy one.

"True as the day is long," assented Derwent. "Yet, I have been a-saving a bolt of rare Highland ewe's wool, dark as a starless sky and cozy as a summer's eve. 'Twill suit well, think I, a person of thy stature and wear well enow besides to enrobe thee many a year hence.

"Act now and (as thou art such a distinguished personage) I shalt add, for a mere pfennig or twain more, velvet trim upon the sleeves and an ermine lining for the hood, such as would warm a Hanseatic trader a-roaming the steppes of Finland. All this shall I personally cut and stitch and sew bespoke to thee and thee alone."

Not long did the stranger mull the crafty tailor's offer afore he rejoined: "'Tis not my practice to barter; yet, I do confess I am in need of what thou suggests. How much time must I grant thee?"

"Oh, not long, not long," assured Derwent. "Concern thyself not with that now. I shalt make a hasty end to this brocade job of work this very eve and put thy cloak the morrow first and foremost amongst all my labors 'til 'tis done."

And with that, the deft tailor did measure and mark the skeletal figure from dark head to darker toe, hip and shoulder until his ebon cloak was be-snowed with tailor's chalk.

"Be certain of thy return in a week and a day for thy first fitting," called out Derwent as the stranger hastened off into the pitch of night.

At the same dark hour one week and a day thereafter, the dark visitor again stood in the little tailor's doorway. "Is it ready?" said he, "for here am I, as bid."

"Ah; come in, come in, good sir; but do watch thy pate. I have cut the wool to measure and now shall we see how it drapes upon thy lank frame."

Derwent threw the cloth over the shoulders of the stranger and set to work with his tailor's twine and chalk. Impatiently the while, the drear customer tapped his boney toes and drummed his boney fingers.

Shortly, Derwent stood and said: "'Twill do for now. Come thee back in but a fortnight and thou shalt behold the goodly shape of things to come."

Stock still and silent stood the tailor's dark guest for a moment. Then said he: "Little tailor, I know not what game thou playest at, but I canna wait upon these new weeds forever. There be those who closely watch o'er all I do, and much have I to do afore I rest."

"Good sir, 'tis no game but the normal course of tailoring. My only object to send thee forth in the finest hood and cloak the world has yet to see. Something that befits a person of your importance. By-the-by, might I suggest that ye consider a drop or two of *eau de toilette*? This old rag of thine has a most unpleasant smell. I hear tell that the ladies in particular do prefer a more sweet-smelling gallant."

"I shall return in a fortnight, as thou sayst," said the dark one ominously; "but I must warn thee . . ."

"Fear not; fear not," interposed Derwent. "I feel thy keen anxiety and most eager am I to complete this task. Thy complete satisfaction is my only goal, I assure thee."

Thus passed one fortnight and then another. Those not too ale-addled in the Swan and Duck might espy a tall, hooded stranger pass down the narrow alley and stoop beneath the low lintel of Derwent the Tailor's humble shop. After but a heartbeat or two, this fearsome figure would again sweep by the alehouse window and disappear once more into the darkness.

On went the fittings and on, as the artful tailor fretted and fumed over the beautiful ebon cloak and hood that seemed ne'er to conform properly to the angular frame of his customer. One time, the hem was not true. Another, a sleeve was too short; the next, 'twas too long. The ermine refused to lie comfortably against the ashen cheek of

Derwent's glum guest. Nor was Derwent content with the seams of the yoke, which had to be stitched and restitched yet again.

And then, more than a year after this work had begun, the dark stranger appeared before his tailor one final time.

"Good and patient sir," began Derwent, "I be certain this time that I have the seams all sewn true and the drape just so. . ."

"Hold!" shouted the figure. "Enough! For I perceive the game thou be playing, and I salute thy craftiness."

"Game, sir?" said the careful tailor, in a voice all innocent and pained.

"Aye," replied the dark figure. "Merry be the chase thou hast led me on and bested me well in the course of it thou hast. 'Tis chess I am master of—if games I do play— and so hereby I resign from the field, leaving thee to rejoice in thy triumph."

Then the clever tailor smiled to himself. "As thou wisheth, honored sir," said he. "And, wilt thou be taking with thee this rare garment that I have so toiled upon, lo these many months gone?"

"That I will," said the grim apparition, "for dearly hath it cost me and 'twill serve to remind me ne'er to put faith in crafty tailors again."

Then the somber figure wrapped his bespoke cloak about him, took up his fearsome crook and said: "Little tailor, thou shalt not see me again for many a year, but heed thou this: keep close this business betwixt and between thee and me or thou shalt rue thy boastfulness."

"I well understand and agree," replied Derwent with a downcast and modest gaze.

Full thirteen years thereafter did Derwent the Tailor

labor on in the shadows of his little shop. Whilst his fingers worked busily, stitching silver bells to the velvet shoes of jesters, fine fur cuffs upon the sleeves of ladies' gowns and embroidered codpieces to the breeches of proud dandies, his mind ranged far and wide o'er loves and laughter long lost.

Nor, at times, could Derwent help but chuckle at the memory of his lank visitor, stalking the dark alley behind the Swan and Duck in a cloak of uneven sleeves, its ermine hood facing rearward and its raveled hem catching up at his heels, whilst tailor's chalk flew from his shoulders like the feathery snow that swirls off a wind-swept scarp.

Tale the Next
Lay of the Lady Randal

Laird Randal took him a young wife, and a fair wife was she. Where he was January, all hoar and ice, she was the twelfth of May, with locks of flax and the southern seas agleam in her eyes of grey.

Not a year and a month of sun and rain were gone before the heart of this fair lady restive grew, and she 'gan cast her lustrous gaze o'er the easeful gallants in her laird's hall. Young were they and with vigor filled; their beards were crisped, their teeth like pearls. Bright hued their cloaks and feathers gay, and comely was their silken hose.

The Lady Randal smiled on the courtier with the velvet cap. To him of plum-dyed cape, she gave her dainty hand. Sat she down to dine nigh him that wore his hair French-cropped and leaned in to hear the one with flowery breath whisper a jaunty tale into her dainty ear.

Before her looking-glass of gilt, the Lady Randal sat her down, combing out her golden braids. "They love me, one and all," quoth she. "Nor can they blamèd be. For, as the honeysuckle draws the bee, so do I lure the men; and, will-I, nil-I, must I lead them on a merry chase."

Then forth went she, both day and eve, coy smiles and looks all bold bestowed both left and right, both fore and aft, 'til her laird spoke thus at last unto this lady wife:

"My dear, I do desire that thou less for'ard be with them at court. Dost thou not see that some may read thy chaste intent amiss?"

"I knowst not what thou means, my laird," rejoined that lady proud. "'Tis but my nature to be blithe with all and one; and kindness I repay with kindness. Would thou have me be another way?"

"Nay," sighed the greybeard laird, "Nay. But pray recall—'tis I thy husband am."

"Oh, well aware of that am I," said that proud lady then, and as she left, twitched up her silver gown.

But still, her laughter and her proffered arm, her smiles and whispers too, abated not a whit. In truth, those manners seemed to grow apace 'til tongues were set a-wagging all through the laird's wide realm.

Nor did this beauteous lady find cause to mend her ways. "'Tis but Nature's gift. Dote on me they must and pursue me still they shall," she said unto her looking-glass. "A merry chase to pass an idle afternoon 'tis all it is, and naught shall come of it!"

More wroth the laird then grew and roared he for his page. "Hie thee, Timothy, and fetch the old crone from out the forest deep wherein she dwells. Most eager am I to plot with her and set this matter right."

That selfsame night, a crooked shadow leaning 'pon its stick crept through the castle gate, and sat it down with that ire laird in consult, close and deep.

"What canst thou do to blind her eyes to all but me alone? And bind her heart likewise to me, her husband dear, so chosen now to be?" So pled the jealous laird.

The eld one pondered a moment's time ere answered him she did: "To steer the heart of woman or man from its instinctive course I cannot do. Nor may I shift the currents that ebb and flow within our restless breasts. My poor powers extend not so far nor so deep. Alas, My Liege, thy lady wife will be as she will be, no matter what we wish."

"Why then, my fury must find a vent lest I become a laughingstock and cuckold in the world's eyes," roared that laird in rage.

Whereat, the ancient hag did sigh: "Beware, I pray, for it is said: A Pure Heart is like an empty bowl; and that which will hold love will hold the other passions, too. Therefore, say I, do have a care, for I must do as thou doth wish, whatever its full effects may be."

"I reck them not," replied the laird. "My heart is stone; and like stone my feelings be 'gainst her and all her train. Do as I wish, and let my wrath upon them fall, come whate'er may."

The Lady Randal rose that morn and sat before her shining glass. A scarf of bright, new silk she twined into her flaxen tresses fair, whilst gaily she did sing: "Desired am I, both wide and far, that no one can gainsay. And all I meet do follow me with eye, and heart and mind."

Just then, she felt a flinty fastness fall upon her limbs, and sinewy did her slender arms and legs become. As dark and vast as the night sky her grey eyes grew, whilst all along her pale skin appeared a russet down; and from her forehead proud there grew two tiny velvet horns.

Nor was this transformation strange all that came to be that morn.

The gallants who had disported once in Laird Randal's splendored hall, were now a roiled pack of hounds baying to be loosed.

Then unto our wondering eyes a fine, red hind burst forth. With velvet horns and dainty hooves, a scarf of silk she wore. And, as she fled through forest green and barren fell, this hind look't back to see the frantic hounds that, without pause, pursued her breathlessly.

Atop the castle ramparts proud, a flinty gargoyle sits. Its heart's of stone; its eyes blink not, but bear their endless witness to the frantic chase below.

Tale the Fourteenth
A Sad Cap in Sooth

When Bjorn and Hans arrived from o'er the Northern Straits, no one—not even Selma, our Village Seer—foresaw what would befall. For, were their ways not foreign and did we not doubt whether we understood their Nordic tongue aright?

The twain set quickly about their business, trapping and flaying the badgers, ferrets and stoats that in those days roamed our fields and raided our hen houses, stitching their pelts into wondrous caps of fur with ingenious flaps to shelter ears 'gainst winter's sleet and wind.

As oft it falls out where two brothers are concerned, Bjorn and Hans differed as rock doth from cloud. Hans was fair of hair and smooth of chin, with eyes as blue and empty as a summer's sky. Tall and well-knit was he, whilst his elder brother was as dark as he was stout and low of stature. Hans had, in sooth, received all the beauty his parents could bestow; yet had he not the brains to fill a cuckoo's pate. Those and more had gone to the swarthy brother, Bjorn, along with a great, ruddy nose and a furry back.

These brothers arrived in April, when new green was every branch and flowering every bough, and ice did not prevent their bark from crossing river and sea. 'Twas not a time of year when we villagers desired caps of fur to shield our pates and ears.

One moonlight night, the brothers sat stitching hides into the caps they fain wouldst sell that over morrow at market. Within his restless brain, Bjorn did weigh whether or no to sail home, where the year 'round, burgher and herder, farmer and fisherman, man, woman and child alike did wear caps with flaps of fur.

This tedious while, Hans fell a-dozing in the warmth of the springtime eve; and though his clear eyes were closed, nonetheless did his manly fingers continue their task apace, as they had been sternly taught.

Bjorn then rounded on his fair brother, desirous of questioning him whether to go or to stay, when his quick, dark eye alighted upon the labor of Hans's heedless hands.

"Thou blockhead!" thundered Bjorn. "Thou dunderhead! Thou ass! Look on that which thou hast wrought! 'Tis without debate or question the saddest cap e'er sewn. Would that I had stout cudgel to hand, thou doltish block of salt!"

Sadly did Hans then peer at his handiwork—and 'twas, in sooth, the saddest cap he e'er had sewn. Its pelts were stitched together some fur-to-the-inside and some fur-to-the-outside. More, there was a third ear flap sewn to the fore and a fourth flap stitched to the back, each with its chin-strap of leather adangle.

"Thou calf!" Bjorn raged on. "Not only hast thou wasted this eve's work, but thou hast ruined these many fine pelts of ermine and ferret. Thou stick! For this thou shalt wear thy handicraft to market on the over morrow so the village entire may bear witness to thy folly and mock thee for it."

Nor could Hans's scalding tears, nor all his pleas, nor any of his apologies dissuade his o'er wroth brother. "Woe is me," wailed poor Hans; "so shalt I the village's laughingstock become as soon as cometh the over morrow." And hard did his slumbers come, both that night and the next.

It so fell out upon next market day that Hans did trudge through the village square in his truly sad cap, piebald in fur and leather, with its four flaps tied snug by their leathern straps 'neath his downy chin.

Ne'er had village man nor village child witnessed so rare a sight. Some gazed in wonder; some laughed aloud; some averted their eyes for fear of giving offence, as round market square Hans and Bjorn paraded with their caps of fur upon a pole. The village swains that lolled beside the Swan and Duck did say: "Sure enow, there goeth a great fool in a fur and leathern cap on this merry spring day."

And yet, every village lass did most willingly follow Hans in his sad cap of ill-stitched leather and fur, calling out his name and entreating his attention. And, like also did the village matrons, whispering and cooing languorous promises as he paced by them.

"Exceeding handsome is he," sayeth one. "Must be that

most rare cap upon his comely head."

"'Tis virile, the likes of which I aint never seen," quoth another.

"Oh, but he must be a most artistic and sensitive fellow," sighed a third.

"'Tis but a sign of his great wisdom and humor," purred a fourth, gazing after the blushing young man.

Hans's sky-blue eyes grew wide and quickened he his pace. Wider still grew the crafty, dark eyes of Bjorn, and into them stole a gleam of clever light.

But widest of all grew the eyes of we village men and lads, for ne'er had seen we our womenfolk so buxom and bestirred.

"It must be that cap that looks so sad atop his head," said one of us.

"Aye; 'tis without a doubt the cap what does it," opined another.

"I must needs buy me one such," vouchsafed a third; "else will pretty Polly heed me not, though fain would I lay me down afore her feet and die."

"And I also," said another and another—and so added I.

In but a fortnight, every village lad and master sported a piebald cap of fur and leather with four sad earflaps tied atop or 'neath a grizzled chin. And, the few furrèd creatures yet dwelling in our fields, woods and fells did then cower deeper within their burrows.

"List thou now, my dear, dull and exceedingly handsome brother," said Bjorn thoughtfully. "Have we not sold thy saddest of all caps to everyone within this village and county 'round? Therefore, either must we find some new ware to peddle or return to the land of ice and snow, richer and wiser though we be."

Now, Hans and Bjorn were loath to flee the warmth of our summer or leave the lovely ladies and lasses of our village just yet, if ye wish to know the truth.

So, Bjorn pondered a while in a brown study, whilst Hans let the cool waters of a freshet lave over and 'round his alabaster ankles.

"Oho and *eureka*!" exclaimed his brother at last. "Have it, I do! If our problem be but that we have slaked the villagers' thirst for caps, why do we not craft bodkins of leather and fur to match 'em? And then, mayhap, buskins of leather with fur-trimmed laces and mayhap e'en bodices of leather and fur for the more daring of them ladies?"

"Uh-mmm," replied Hans, his mind as empty of thoughts as a deserted croft.

"And..." continued Bjorn excitedly, "shalt thou not, my simple but exceptionally attractive brother, trod forth in each new garment for all the village to see and to admire? Oh, reason not their needs, Dear Dullard; 'tis but their fears and desires we stitch onto their hearts; and the thirsts we create in their simple breasts, so also shall we slake at the same time."

That very eve, the brothers twain set their ingenious gin to work, stitching attire of leather and fur the likes of which the world—or leastways our village—had ne'er seen.

Ever and anon, Hans did then stroll through our marketplace, fitted out in fur and leather that gladdened the eyes of our womenfolk; whilst we men, young and old, coursed after Bjorn, jingling our ducats and pfennigs down to the very last farthing, that we might be as fashionably attired as was this marvelous Hans.

And e'en though the September sun held warm and bright that year—and e'en though we sweated rivers thereat—natheless did we, man and boy, girl and goodwife, walk about be-furrèd and be-leathered in boots and vests and hats and cloaks until we seemed the hairiest beasts left in the forest.

Throughout the county wide and far, let others laugh and jibe. We care not a fig—for, are we not, summer, spring, winter and fall, the very masters and mistresses of our own, new fashion?

Tale the Fifteenth
The Jolly Highwaymen and the Crone

Dejected sat the two highwaymen, Dinkin and Lesley, beside the crooked track that ran through the deep, dark forest. For they had labored, both night and day, and had taken nothing.

"'Tis far more difficult than e'er I imagined," moaned Lesley, mopping his sunburnt brow.

"'Tis because thou knowst not what thou be about, thou blockhead!" uttered Dinkin, with ruddy cheek and blazing eye. "First must thou shout 'Stand!' in a voice of thunder, and only then sayeth 'Deliver,' thou empty reed. Thou hast all the brains of an ant, I ween."

"Nay, cousin. 'Deliver' be the main point of it all. What care we if they cast their pearls afore us and flee or if they bring forth their treasure with trembling hands and rooted foot? *Sans* they deliver, what hath we gained?"

reasoned Lesley. "Ah, woe is us—how could things go more amiss?"

"Thou couldst be seated in poison oak, as I see thou art," observed Dinkin with a weary sigh.

That very morning, the twain had crouched amidst the thorns and brambles that grow thick beside the bending path, when there came a gilded carriage with a gilded lord sitting therein, feasting on candied figs. Of gold were the chains he wore; crusted with jewels were the rings upon his sticky fingers. His sapphire cloak was of the finest satin, and bright buckles of polished silver adorned his silk slippers.

"Deliver!" shouted Lesley, leaping from behind a mulberry bush.

"Nay," shouted Dinkin. "Stand first! Then deliver."

"Drive on, driver," bid the gilded lord in a loud, bored voice. "These varlets be but paltry poltroons that know not what they be about."

Thereupon, the haughty coachman did click his tongue and shout "Hie!" The brace of silver-white chargers pricked up their ears and away the carriage did fly, but not before it bowled o'er the highwaymen like two badly marred duckpins.

Battered were Dinkin and Lesley, and, in sooth, more bruised than battered were their spirits.

"Mayhap we should return us to our village and resume our labors there," lamented Lesley.

"Oh, ye of little hope," sneered Dinkin. "Loathe am I to lug a hod about or e'er again sweep streets with a broom of vile straw! 'Tis but a matter of time afore we fall upon riches untold."

For, Dinkin was mindful still of the lovely lady who'd

come a-riding all lost and 'lone not two days before.

"Stand!" had he shouted in a voice like thunder.

"And deliver," had Lesley added, leaping like a djinn from amidst the briars that twine within the shadowy wood.

"Pray, my good fellows, harm me not, for I be but a maid all innocent, bereft in this world and on a desperate errand of love."

"Reck we not," Dinkin had replied. "For, have we not great hunger ourselves and great need of those pearls thou hast about thy alabaster neck and that jewel-encrusted tiara that nestles there amidst those amber tresses of thine?"

"Aye; and forget not those rings of silver and of gold that adorn thy delicate, ivory fingers and most slender toes," had Lesley put in, somewhat shyly.

"Kind sirs," had the maiden then replied, "all that and more wouldst I give ye, had ye but a bag or carryall in which to bear it off."

Dumbstruck, the hapless highwaymen had then looked at one another and then down at their empty hands.

"And now, no longer may I tarry here in this dank place; for, I must away to court and there lay claim to my dear lord, whom I have loved since I were but a lass. Yet, has he not abandoned me to shame and sorrow, and I all great with his child?" At which words, a crystalline tear had coursed down her cream-white cheek.

Then had Dinkin stepped aside, saying: "Do pass by unharmed, fair maid, and Godspeed to thee; for though we be but thieves and ruffians, we be not villains." Low had he bowed before her, pulling the gape-mawed Lesley from the maiden's path. Off had she pranced then upon her grey gelding, gaily singing "tra-la, tra-la, tra-la" as lightly on she rode.

E'en now could Dinkin hear her silver laugh echo through the wood, while the feckless thieves had stood, empty of hand, athwart the twisty, narrow path.

"Alas," moaned Lesley, interrupting Dinkin's morose reverie. "'Tis starting to rain. What a misery of brigands we art."

"Do hush thy whining," replied Dinkin, "do I not hear someone a-coming?"

'Twas true. From out the forest gloom, there came a bullfrog's voice singing a weird chantey of wind and storm and moon and stars. In a trice, there appeared a stooped figure, leaning on a stick of yew wood and wrapped from toe to head in robes and scarves the hue of coal, whilst toting an old canvas sack upon its shoulder.

"Deliver!" shouted Lesley, violently scratching at his itching arms and backside.

"Nay, stand thou fast first and then deliver," corrected Dinkin, his voice also like thunder.

Up looked the face of the traveler...and 'twas that of an agèd crone, wrinkled and blear of eye, yet with a small smile upon her crinkled lips.

"Gladly wouldst I deliver, save possessions have I none," said this beldame.

"Then what be in that sack thou dost carry?" demanded Lesley.

"Why, 'tis empty as e'er be the dreams of an old woman," replied the hag.

"Hand it over and we'll not harm thee," said Dinkin; "for we are in need of somewhat in which to carry off our pelf."

"From what I hear," muttered she, "ye have little enow of that. This empty sack is all ye need, though ye knowst it not."

Yet, hand it over she did, adding aloud, "'Tis a lesson all must learn: take only what is needful and beware of a-hungering for more." Then off stalked the old woman, back into the dim forest from whence she came.

"What a strange, eld hag was she," said Lesley, scratching at his spotty arms and legs.

Anon, there came along the twisted way a merchant from the town. Plump was he as a Saint's Day goose, and bags of gold hung from his belt like ripe pears from a bough.

With the fierceness of lions did the two highwaymen spring forth, demanding that the merchant stand and deliver there and then. Watched they with eager eyes as his trembling hands dropped bag after bag of coin and jewels and chains of rare metal into the old crone's sack. Then flew they like the wind unto a secret lea, wherein Lesley fell upon the ground scratching himself and laughing aloud.

Peering into the old woman's sack to tally up what all they had taken, Dinkin did exclaim: "Why, 'tis empty! What hath become of our hard-earned pelf?"

"Mayhap the old woman's bag hath a hole innut," ventured Lesley.

"Thinkst thou so?" exclaimed Dinkin, "thou wickless candle, thou heap of sodden kindling!" Yet, seek as he might, nor hole nor rent in that old sack could he find.

"Hallo! What have we here?" sayeth Dinkin then, as out from the hag's bag's recesses, he pulled a roast of beef and a pot of mustard. "Ah, well. Ne'er look a gift goat in the eye 'til thou taste the stew, as they say."

"Do they now?" puzzled Lesley. The two highwaymen then fell upon their repast without further word as vultures fall upon fresh carrion.

From that day forth, did the careers of Lesley and Dinkin as brigands and thieves take wing. They robbed princes and princesses, burghers and clowns, abbots and freeholders, one and all. Yet, from their pilferer's sack poured not diamonds nor pearls, gold nor silver, ducats nor gilders, but banquets of venison and ham and beef and ale and sweet fruit and desserts of honey and milk instead.

Fat grew the twain and more sanguine Dinkin's temper grew as well, 'til the two became known both wide and far as the *Jolly Highwaymen*, ever courteous and gentle as they preyed upon unwary travelers.

And, all the while, deeper within the forest, the sly old dame did smile and hum her wild sea chanteys, as both day and night the Jolly Highwaymen's pelf appeared heaped upon her doorstop—whence 'twas quickly whisked into her burgeoning storerooms with great and tender care.

Ƈale the Sixteenth
Ballade of Star Bright

"**Be thou my bride** and pole star bright, and I shall care for thee. 'Tis all I ask, or e'er shall want," firm Will doth swear upon their wedding day.

"So promise I and so I'll do," Star Bright plights back. "To thee and all thy kinfolk 'round. I promise all thou doth desire. Yet, I shall do what more I can, for thou my husband art, and I, come good or ill, thy helpmate am."

"Naught need I save thy steadfast light, and all the rest shall I achieve," stern Will repeats. "No more's required of thee."

The morning next, Will doth depart into the world of men. He pauses at his cottage door to tell Star Bright: "Bide here but for a while, my trusted and my only wife, for thy sure beams must guide me home when I our fortune's made."

Then tight he bolts that cottage door, so very proud is he.

Long sits Star Bright beside her hearth, and long she waits for his return. At last, she hears his footstep slow, and up leaps she in joy, her dear Will there to greet.

But all Will says is this: "Leave be, won't thou? The world hath badly treated me, and weary to the bone I be."

A week of stormy days in silence dawdle by, ere once again stanch Will sets out, his fortune for to seek.

As pale novices do wait in deference to their vows, so there in silence Star Bright shines. And prays she not, as novices do, that Will good fortune finds? Alas, good fortune fails her darling Will to find.

Time and again, the World proves cruel; time and again, Will's schemes do wilt like morning blooms in noonday's hotter suns.

At last, Star Bright pleads to her Will: "My husband true, here I bide beside our hearthstone fire as but a vessel all forgot. Do thou let me, thy helpmate fit, to smooth thy way, for I am strong and can do much, whate'er be the labor."

At her fair hope, doth Will but glower at their garden wall. In scorn and anger, he replies: "Dost thou not recall what I of thee had asked—that thou remain my guiding star, whilst I our fortunes proved? Hast thou forgot thy wedding vows, soon as these ills have come?"

Again, doth fickle Fortune call him forth, and again doth Will her follow. On winter seas, where storms do rage, his frail bark seeks harbor. Through wind and wave and ice and all, is Star's bright name upon his lips, and ever in his mind, the promises they once had made.

Comes Will to port at last, and up Star Bright doth

spring, her weary seaman to embrace and welcome safely home. Yet, troubled still is Will's dark brow, and weary of the tossing seas is he. And still the ceaseless waves do pound within his stubborn breast.

"Alas, dear man," sighs Star Bright then. "What boots thy toil if I lend not the help thou needs nor succor thee when day is done? Nor do I care to sit here all day beside our humble hearth when there is work that I could do, and much I do desire."

Wroth grows Will to hear her thoughts, and in hot anger shouts, "Vowed we not, that sun-bright morn, to mind our wedding troth? All they asked—and little it was— that thou should light my way as any taper might, though dark the night might be. Thou promised me thy help would ne'er fade, regardless of the winter snows or rain or winds that came."

Strict Will looks to their garden wall once more, where Star's pea vines do bloom, and not word more speaks he to her nor looks he at his wife.

The morrow next, rash Will enlists, and marches forth in his red coat. From garden's gate, Star Bright doth watch, as the crimson ranks tramp by.

"Huzzah!" she bravely cheers, "And here shalt thou find me, in vespers shadows or the blaze of noon, it matters not to me."

"See 'tis so, my only Star, for I shall think of thee," Will says and grimly, too—and then his heartless sergeant cries, "March on, me lads, march on!"

In bloody fields, where many do fall to War's steel scythe and sword; and many 'round faint Will lie dead, poor Will prays to the sky: "Shine bright, my love, and be there shining still,'til I return or, if Fate wills, 'til this, my life, is through."

In five years' time, Will once more appears within their garden green, now bearded like a bear; and all about he sees the fruits of Star Bright's labors' care—the blooms upon the garden wall, the sheaves she's gathered in, the well-fed flocks, and silver coins that all about the cottage lie.

Up wells his anger at these fair sights, as typhoons swell upon the seas; and through his anger and his scorn, all haughtily he cries: "Was this the *all* I asked of thee? 'Tis I who've kept our nuptial vows, and I who've kept 'em true. All that thou hast here achieved tells me thou durst not say the same!"

"Dear sir, my promise I've kept—and more," a tearful Star replies. "For, e'en as thou standeth there, in thy sorry coat of red, have I not saved a hearth for thee that's warm, a harbor safe and calm?"

"Far from thy wedding vows that is," scowls Will, glowering at their cottage wall. "Far is it from the only thing I asked of thee on that one day or since!"

"Canst thou not take what I've become?" then cries the anguished Star. "As the brightest star doth rise and fade in the heavens above, so changeth all that dwells here below. Like that star and all that lives, we each do change and grow."

"Fie say I," swears stony Will. "Thou promised my sole guide to be in foreign fields and unknown seas. And, though the battle confusèd be, thy steadfast light would keep me safe, whate'er Fortune's plan. Where be that light, where be thy vows, now thou hast changèd so?"

At this, doth poor Star Bright consider in her heart: "'Tis Will I love and always shall; yet his love's a dungeon drear, so closed about and without light I cannot breathe therein.

"What I would be and what I am are not what he desires. See I, instead, that we must part lest we become as drowning sailors who together cling and pull each other down."

Then swears Star Bright unto her Will, "My love and only husband dear, from this day forth my vows I'll keep and see, as best I may, that evermore a star there'll be to light thee on thy way."

That selfsame night, steps Star Bright forth and pauses by her garden gate. Into the heavenly vault above, she hurls the ember bright new stolen from her hearth.

"Thus I do," she murmurs low, "my bridal pledge fulfill." Then off she flees into the night, and no one here knows where.

To this day in heavens above, that glowing ember shines. And some do claim a goodwife dwells not very far from here, whose labors good profits bring, though all alone she dwells.

While his fortunes prosper not, roams he hither or yon, all that weary Will has yet to do is turn his gaze aloft, and that bright star that glimmers there shall quiet his troubled heart.

Tale the Seventeenth
Ten Barrows Lane

As are wind and fire, just so were Yeoman Stefan and Yeoman Carleton, albeit they'd lived beside the selfsame lane that leads into the same dark wood since they were wee lads together. Stout was Yeoman Stefan, with worried eyes of grey and ruddy hair that saw neither comb nor brush. Lithe as a sapling was Yeoman Carleton, and his eyes shone like sapphires.

There they toiled cheek by jowl upon their neighboring plots, planting and reaping and guarding their flocks 'gainst marauders. Yet, their farmstead husbandry differed as day from night. Scythe and crook and hammer and basket did each pend from its appointed peg upon the new-painted wall of Stefan's cottage; whilst in Carleton's farmyard, all lay ajumble where it fell; nor couldst thou find nail nor pitch nor thatch to patch his cot's leaking roof.

"Ah, but it leaks not when the sun doth shine," said Carleton with hearty cheer as he reposed in the shade of a willow tree. "Why clamber upon yon heights when, like as not, my ladder will not bear me safely up nor down, nor will I able be to find the leak when 'tis bone dry?"

Thereat Stefan sighed a heavy sigh and turned to harry the few, rash weeds that dared to raise their timid heads midst his vegetables and then to trim close his side of the hedgerow that grew high and thorny betwixt their two yards.

"Think thou beyond today, shouldst thou not, my good neighbor?" observed sweating Stefan sourly. But, Carleton was by then napping, a chapbook of idylls open upon his lap, and he heard Stefan not.

Anon, each young man did take a wife. Stefan cleaved unto the pale Parsimonia for his sour helpmeet. And, all we folk here 'round said "Parsa" was a fair and buxom choice; for well could she govern hearth and chicken shed alike.

Carleton the while, plighted troths with the flighty Ludicity—she that loved naught more than to sing and dance the night long in the Swan and Duck. And all here 'round said "Ludie" was the bride we expected Yeoman Carleton to wed.

For three years and a day did the gentle seasons favor freeholder, tenant and herdsman. Came the rains when rains were needed; shone the sun when shine it ought; calm and pleasant passed winter's days.

In those good times, Yeoman Stefan and Goodwife Parsa did store up with great care the fruits of their toil, and more. Laid they by bushels of grain and bales of hay and rashers of bacon and wheels of cheese. Parsa patched their clothes 'til they were more patches than whole cloth.

Stefan sowed and reaped and painted and pruned, all in a heat; and they did eat but one meal a day and drink of naught but water. On a high shelf in the corner of their cot, Parsa kept a dusty jar filled with pfennigs saved and pfennigs earned.

In due time, Parsa gave birth unto a child. They christened him "Little Jack," and from his earliest day, a careworn lad was he: a squirreler away of crusts of bread and bits of cheese 'gainst the time when the font of these viands should fail.

Carleton watched his neighbors' lives from the easeful bower of his willow tree, where he and Ludie took the summer's shade, reading poetry and sipping sweet, windfall wine.

"Go thou more slow, my dripping friend, for the Good Lord's sake," Carleton called out. "For, be not the fruits of our labors there for the savoring? What boots it to scrimp thy wife and Little Jack in such manner? Are not the sun warm and the meadows lush? And yet thou flailest away withal as at a stubborn mule. Come join us. I have wine enow to quench thy thirst as the heat of noon comes on."

Stefan glared across the thorny hedge at Carleton's slovenly yard, tare-filled crops, tattered cottage and unwashed children five playing in the dirt, and eyed he, too, dozing Ludie; and all he looked upon did sore offend his stern, grey eye.

"Nay, good neighbor," replied Stefan dourly. "In this world, toil is our lot and *provide* we must. If that means but Sweat and Worry, why then, be it so. Nor will the sun shine always nor the rains be e'er to time. The World is indifferent to our wants, I ween, and so must we strive constantly 'gainst it." Then, returned he to his hard labors all the more determined.

"As you please, dear neighbor. Yet I fear thou shalt work thyself into an early grave," observed Carleton blandly.

Then came three years and a day of drought and heat and cold and crops that withered and kine that died standing upright in the sleet of winter storms.

Anon, Yeoman Carleton and Goodwife Ludie found that their cupboard and larder were bare. They had eked out a living when times were good; yet now, Ludie's locks were grown lank and thin, and tattered were her sateen gowns. Glumly sat their children five on the stoop of their leaking cottage, too forlorn e'en to whimper for their suppers.

Then did Carleton call across the thorny hedgerow, "Dear neighbor, prithee lend me but a bit of that grain and a tranche or two of that cheese thou hast laid by; for, zounds, how we be suffering now, lacking groat or farthing."

"That do be a pity, my dear neighbor," answered Stefan. "But 'twould not be prudent to do aught. For neither I nor thou canst know for certain when—if e'er—this hard run of foul weather shalt end and crops and herds and hens and gardens flourish again. In such times as these, I trow, 'tis every man—and woman and child—for himself."

At this haughty answer Carleton grew wroth: "Well thou knowst that were the sabot upon the other foot, nor Ludie nor I would hesitate a cat's wink to share with thee and thine. Whence cometh this cold heartlessness?"

"'Tis not coldness, neighbor, but justice simple and pure. For, well did I observe the times ye spent idling in the shade of yon willow and also in the Swan and Duck a-swilling, both thou and thy feckless wife."

"Thou and thine were invited. Oft." argued Carleton. "'Tis neither fair nor just to throw that up 'gainst us now."

"Must the World be just or fair?" reasoned Stefan loftily. "Thou wert e'er a lazy beggar. I must tend to mine own and thee to thine, e'en though thou hast chosen to lie upon a bed wherein there be but little straw."

"Thou wretched puritan," exploded Carleton then. "'Tis but love of thine own virtue that governs thee now!" And grabbed he up a clot of dried earth, which he hurled at Stefan.

Thereat, Stefan did return the favor—and more. In a trice, the air was filled with shoes and knives and clots of dirt and goat dung and foul eggs and fouler words, as Stefan, Parsa and Little Jack battled valiantly 'gainst the fierce assault of Carleton, Ludie and their five desperate kinder.

'Midst this terrible tumult, not one of the combatants espied the somber figure that came hobbling down the lane on a wooden stick.

"Well, well, well. Here be a fine battle royal, I be bound," said the old hag as near she drew. "I ha' not seen such a dustup since my good man, Dennis the djinn, set the two Eastern princelings at one another's throats, thereby bringing peace unto their realm."

Then called she out: "Arrest and halt ye, one and all, so that your elder (I say not your better, mind) may safely pass!"

"You there, Yeoman Carleton," shouted she.

"Admirable is thy faith in the world's goodness, and through it, you have prospered at times, I trow. Yet, are ye not like the bright-hued flowers in June that bloom but briefly beside a freshet stream? As the spring's grass doth green 'neath winter's snows and good cider tasteth best once harvest is safe home, so we our pleasures must take in their due course, and in that measure dance a stately *pavane* for our lives."

"And you, Yeoman Stefan," continued this old philosopher. "Take especial care lest of thy o'er-heated virtues thou dost make thee into a smithy forge, one that smelts thy soul to cold steel and burns thy heart to but a cinder. For, which of us can say for certain sure: 'No need hath I now or e'er of aid from friend or neighbor?'"

"Tut, tut, ye twain, tear down this thorny hedge and dwell henceforth as good neighbors ought."

Like statues carved of stone stood the ten combatants. Agape were their mouths and fixèd their eyes upon the ancient orator.

Of a sudden, Little Jack cried: "Be that as it may, not a one of those lazy takers shalt have crumb nor jot o' my bread and cheese!" And, he hurled a goat turd so that it smote poor Ludie full upon her balding pate.

"Well tossed, my pretty lad," murmured Parsa.

On the instant, was the air filled once again with curses and sticks and ordure, as neighbors rich and poor alike fell to 'gainst one another. Seeing this, the old woman shrugged and hobbled off down the lane, muttering a curse upon both their houses.

To this very day, shouldst thou venture down Ten Barrows Lane, there shalt thou see ten tumuli of refuse and earth and stone ranged seven and three astride an o'ergrown hedge.

Some claim that if thou harken close, thou shalt hear an angry muttering within those ancient mounds; and few—save schoolboys upon a dare—do trod upon those ten hillocks without a sudden frost befalling their anxious hearts.

Tale the Eighteenth
The Laughing Babe

As Midwife Marjorie gladly would tell any and all: "A bairn that's born into this world enters it a-cryin'—'tis the gift of Father Adam and Mother Eve; and, aye, the wee ones knows it."

This truth was true as rain and sun for all save one— the bonny babe born unto the village smithy and his wife full sixteen years and a day gone by. "Jesper" they named him; and he came into this world with laughter burbling from his lips like water from a wellspring.

"Ne'er have I seen the like in all my years of birthin'," Marjorie exclaimed. "Sure now, this 'un bears close watchin'!"

Only two days and a week old was Jesper when Squinty Tom did ogle him as he lay toying with his toes amidst his swaddling clothes. The tiny bairn stared up into old Tom's twisty face for but a moment's time, and, sure as jonquils amid the melting snow, did slowly close his blue left eye and prune out his wee pink lips.

"See there how he apes thee now!" shouted the smithy with glee. "'Tis the very image of thyself, Thomas—all toothless, bald and squint-eyed." Father Ignatius, Dame Deiter, and Goodwife Sally did join in the hearty laughter at the babe's bald jest.

"That 'er boy bears watchin'," said Squinty Tom, in hot anger. "Such sass shalt do him ill when he be a babe namore." And full of wrath, he stomped out of the smithy's door.

As grass grows in the meadows of July, Jesper did sprout; and all in the village soon learned of his marvelous skill at apery. For, little Jesper was adept in mime and mimicry like none before or none thereafter.

When but a lad of seven, he could mime Sam'el the Seaman, who dozed beside the Swan and Duck, an empty tankard adangle from his drowsy fingers and his head a-loll upon his stained sea-coat. Staggered little Jesper around his father's forge on bandy legs as on a heaving deck, moaning out sea chanties no man nor wife could understand. "Avast!" "Hold!" "Belay them lines!" would the tiny lad shout and peer about him with befogged gaze, whilst the village laughed itself to tears at Jesper's drunken sailor.

"A clever imp that Jesper be, in sooth! 'Tis the very drunkard hisself," roared they. "That boy bears watchin', 'e does."

So, likewise, Jesper metamorphosed himself into the Widow Wardlowe, who had dwelt hard upon the village green far longer than any could remember. Down bent he his head until his chin all but touched his knees. Upon a gnarled stave of oak he leaned, and glared he up from 'neath his beetled brows at all who crossed his path. "Make way; make way, thou foul slug," growled Jesper. "Respect thou not thine elders?" And off Jesper hobbled, like a hedgehog, a-grumbling to himself.

He mimed the trembling steps of Ancient Gimble, his shanks aquiver and aquake whilst making towards the door in circles, grasping at any shoulder, arm or chair a cat's wink afore he toppled o'er.

He aped the Spinster Tarttapple, screwing up his eyes and mouth 'til they seemed but an autumn's withered windfall. In her peevish voice, complained he high and long of the village layabouts that failed to husband her.

Mimicked Jesper, too, the moon-eyed and slack-jawed tapster's daughter, Lovelorn Lucy, who gawped with lusty longing at all the strapping farm lads quaffing down her father's mead. So distracted was his Lucy that imaginary ale o'erflowed imaginary flagons and ran down her arms into her slop-shod sabots, which Lucy—or rather Jesper— all in a fog of lust, did empty out.

The boy added to his menagerie young Lord Orwent, mincing on tiptoe in sateen slippers through the mud and dung of the marketplace, whilst tugging at his wisp of beard. Mimicked he, too, the Laird Clarendon, he of grasping hands and foul breath, rounding on farm and croft to pick the purses of the weary tenants who worked his stony lands.

When Jesper turned sixteen, he caught the figure and form of Yeoman Ander. Of oxlike build and wit, his legs and arms did shift like ponderous trunks of wood, while his thoughts did move more slow.

"What a roguish knave that Jesper be," some few villagers did say. "Mayhap tomorrow he'll go too far; yet today, 'tis all in fun."

In lodge, farm and hamlet round, Jesper's fame did grow. On market day, he set up a tent and curtain green, and all gathered 'round to see which great or low personage the scamp would strut forth. In riotous chorus, they shouted out the name of each, as forth each figure came; and the more the people laughed, the more did Jesper hone his craft.

Anon, he conjured up Brother Ignatius, fumbling with his psalter and slopping the blood of our Lord o'er the lip of the Holy Chalice. Jesper aped Squire Gregory, carried about in a two-man chair with his gouty foot jutting out like the rotting stump of a chestnut tree, whilst he groaned and moaned of his throbbing head and guts.

At last, to loud laughter and hurrahs, he mimicked the Village Elders three. Each drank deep and scratched an addled pate and drank some more ere each concluded: "Why, there's no help for't. There's nothing left to be done"—and called for another bumper full.

The very next day, these same mocked Elders did hold court in the back chamber of the Swan and Duck, whereto, by twos and ones, irate denizens did traipse.

"'Tis disrespectful of his betters," said one.

"'Tis insulting to us, one and all," insisted another.

"I'll break his bones and smash his pate," vowed Yeoman Ander.

"Did not our Heavenly Father counsel that youth should be the last among us to cast stones?" misquoted Brother Ignatius. "If not, 'twas certainly His meaning."

"The boy stirs insubordination and rebellion," argued

the Laird Lawrence. "For that alone, he bears careful watchin'."

One after another, the villagers complained of the wrongs that Jesper had done them, all the while insisting that they, of course, found the lad's jibes and jests but harmless fun and, in the main, good for morale.

"I suggest we issue a command unto the boy's parents," drawled Elder Crimmons. "For 'tis clear as April's brooks that the lad goeth too far."

"Aye," piped up Elder Mathieus. "But, let us send in our stead the old woman what dwells within the forest. She'll know right how to warn him for good and all."

"Agreed!" chimed in Elder Bramble. "'Twill solve our problems neatly and put an end to this spreading discontent. Yet, ere we proceed, let us call upon buxom Lucy for another round."

So it came to pass that, in but a day and night, the dark figure of the old woman appeared on the threshold of the village smithy and his wife. Nor did she tarry there long.

"We know well what thou hast come for and well who hath dispatched thee here," said the smithy.

"I fear our good citizens be not of the mirror-loving kind," replied this beldame. "They would rather shatter the glass than look upon the image it shows 'em. Albeit, must I confess that the lad's imposture of myself, droll though it may ha' been to some, did seem a tidge or two wide of apt."

Two days thereafter, Jesper staged his last and final show upon the village green. Yet now, the only figure that appeared from behind the curtain was the lad himself, with bowed head, wiping away feigned tears that seemed to flood from sorrow-filled eyes. In his hand he bore a staff of sturdy yew, and on his back he wore a cloak of grey, as he mimed a forlorn walk from his home village into the cold, wide world beyond.

Silent stood the villagers as Jesper turned his dreary pantomime into reality. With steps stately and slow, he trudged down the lane and onto the high road, whilst the smithy and his wife did wave and weep and call "farewell" after their lightsome lad.

As Jesper paced forth, the bright colors from 'round the village did flow after him like the waters of a March torrent. Ran they onto his grey cloak and leggings and shirt and vest until Jesper was like a walking rainbow, as o'er hill and through vale he took his way.

They say that when the King saw Jesper amongst the crowd, he shouted: "Why, what a colorful knave that rascal be! Closely must we watch him! Let him be taken into my court for our Royal Amusement and Good Cheer!"

And that is how Jesper became the King's Jester, he who made the lords and ladies—and e'en the King himself, at times—laugh at the mirror image of themselves his clever foolery held up.

As for the villagers and their dwellings, why, they remained but shades of grey—of ash and stone and cloud and troubled sea and gravestones grave—nor would any color, bright or clear, long endure where laughter at one's self had long ago departed.

Tale the Nineteenth
Prince Charming and His Princess Fair

Griselda and Gretchen, the Glumm sisters, perched in their finery on damask tufts like birds of the New World, sipping spiced wine and feeding on krumkake and sweetmeats.

"Thou shouldst ha' harkened to me," said Griselda, who was lank as a hay rake with a chin like an axe. "Did I not tell thee that thy marriage to the prince would not fadge?"

"Aye," piped up Gretchen, bodied like a pippin with lime-green eyes and wiry orange hair, as she brushed krumkake crumbs from her bosom's tabletop. "Thou, dear sister, wert never right for him. 'Twas fated to end badly. Alas."

At this, the patient Princess Jewel turned her violet eyes to the window. "So said ye both, and oft," sighed she.

"Yet, he was most charming and gay there upon his steed of white in his cloak of royal blue and his silken hose with the silver threads and his chevalier's hat all be-feathered."

"Still and all, he were not for the likes o' thee, my dear," weighed in Mother Glumm. Absently she stroked Pepper, her beady-eyed lap dog, adding primly: "Thou art but a simple country girl, whilst he is of noble breeding. I should ha' insisted he marry our dear Griselda—or even our belovèd Gretchen here—in thy stead. 'Twould have been the better match for all, I ween."

Mother Glumm took a deep draught of spiced wine, settled herself deeper into her cushions, and fed the princess's sweetmeats to Pepper, whose moist eyes glinted like bits of glass.

"All and all, 'tis but water in a weir and naught to be done," concluded Mother Glumm loftily. "The question now is canst thou do aught about it? Husbands be but hounds, I wot, and thou must keep thine fast by his leash least all gang astray."

"And where would that leave us then?" piped up Gretchen, her many chins atremble.

"Aye. On whom could we call of an afternoon or who would then welcome us to their banquets and balls? Far and fast would be our fall wert thou to fail at thy wifely duties," added Griselda with great indignity.

"Jewel, heed your loving sisters," grunted Mother Glumm, as she struggled to rise, "and do whate'er lies within thy ken to preserve our good standing...and thine, of course. Well do I know, for have I not had husbands four?"

Whereat the three Glumms left the palace with great ado to elaborate genuflections from every misfortunate servant unable to evade their haughty progress.

Whereupon, Princess Jewel encountered the Lord Chamberlain Walter, faithful and agèd counselor to kings and queens alike.

"Forgive me, my dear Princess," croaked Walter. "I could not help but overhear. 'Tis true the prince be not now—shall we say—as 'sprightly' as erstwhile. He hath let himself go a trifle since thy nuptials, I do confess.

"But yet, let it not trouble thy pretty head," wheezed windy Walter. "We men be like barnyard dogs that chase after every passing chaise and shay. Loud is our bark and full of high purpose our charge; but little reck we what to do with horse and cart once we ha' caught 'em. No more is there to do then but bark and bray after the next carriage that jolteth by. 'Tis how we pass our days."

Sighed Jewel a heavy sigh and thanked the old lord, regardless of whether his similes were illuminating or not.

On trod she to the chambers of good Queen Beatrice, who sat before her gilded dressing table decorating her hairpiece with ribbons and stuffed birds.

"Ah, my dear daughter-in-law," said the queen. "Come, do sit thee down. And, prithee tell: why such heavy sighs and such wan glances?"

Queen Beatrice did list to dejected Jewel's tale with but half an ear, for she was absorbed in making her diamonds and pearls, ribbons and birds most fit for the banquet of state that evening. When Jewel fell silent, up spoke this much-distracted queen.

"My dear, dear child, fret not. E'er was our prince a moody little chap. Good heavens! Times were when he was more mutable than the moon, nor as predictable. I shouldna worry, were I thou: husbands be a mystery in any case. And besides, is he not yet handsome—albeit with his doublet undone and as oft ill-coiffed as he is nowadays?"

With heavy head and heavier heart, Jewel did trudge on to the Marital Suite, wherein she found her charming prince, much as his mother had lately described him, but also with his silken hose fall'n garterless about his ankles, gazing from the palace window whilst leaning 'pon its sill.

"My darling husband," she ventured, "is there aught that ails thee? Mayn't I be of comfort or solice?"

"Ah, 'tis nothing, my dear bride and love. A mere trifle," sighed the prince. "Not bear-baiting, nor hunting the antler'd hart, nor falconry, nor sword-play, nor country dancing, nor fishing for the plashy trout delights me this day or the 'morrow. The life of a prince proves a rather tedious thing, I find." And, he turned back to the windowsill, whereon he leaned his manly arm and gazed and leaned some more.

Alone and silent sat Jewel in her Robing Room when came there a gentle tap upon her door. Softly entered Jesper, the Court Jester, and tiptoed to her side, his fool's bells a-jingle.

"What is black as pitch yet gives clear light?" whispered he.

"'Tis a riddle too hard for my poor brain," replied Jewel. "A lump of coal, mayhap?"

"Aha! Good answer, good answer," cried Jesper; "I hadna thought o' that! Nay; what I was thinking of was the eld crone what dwells deep within the forest. Many a time and oft have I heard from ladies young and old that 'twas she that lent 'em candlelight for their gloomy and troubled nights. Why, truth to tell, 'tis down to her that I be here at court at all—but that's another tale."

Thus it came to pass that a bent figure with a walking stick cut of yew root and a cloak the color of midnight preceded Jesper into Jewel's Private Chambers late that selfsame night.

"My child," said this old crone to the befuddled princess, "thy be-belled friend here hath told me of thy trials—and oh how familiar they are! Now and then do husbands—and wives, also, I trow—find themselves becalmed upon the troubled seas of life. Nor can we do much to luff the wind back into their limp sails."

"I fear I be no sailor, madam; still, is there nothing to be done?" protested Princess Jewel, a tear coursing down her creamy cheek.

"Canst thou not make him blithe and happy and—at least somewhat—as well-groomed he was? Hast thou no potion or 'cantation to enthrall a prince's heart? Why camest thou here in the thick o' night if all we may do is smile and hope and hope and smile?" she moaned.

"Some mystical tricks I might attempt were the moon now new or full," mused the wizened one. "Natheless, it falls out in the end that each of us must find content within our own, proper hearts; for therein are we each alone our own masters and mistresses.

"Yet, despair not, I beg of thee; and lean in close ye twain, for I have an idea. Knowst ye that we be as the sun and rain to those we love and can make conditions fair or foul for their happiness to blossom? Like diligent gardeners, then, let us cultivate a plot that may yet help yon prince regain his princely vigor."

For an hour—no more, no less—did the three heads lie a-plotting together, at the end of which Jewel exclaimed:

"Why, there be no magic to this at all! 'Tis nothing but gossip and rumor...and...and a mirror."

"No magic, 'tis true; yet the effect may well prove magical," affirmed the crone. "E'en a despondent dog will sometime bay and hunt, if we but loose his tether and steer him in the right direction. Let us set our gin in motion and see if, or how, transformation may sprout."

The morning next, the unkempt prince slouched forth from his Princely Bedchambers. At once, came he upon a mirror of sparkling Venetian glass, newly hung upon the palace wall. Being a charming prince, both well-born and well-bred, what could he do but regard himself therein, and therein note his disordered hair and wolfish beard and stained kerchief and threadbare doublet of fading green velvet?

Nor could he help but wonder at the inscription etched into the mirror's gilt frame:

Who Wilt Thou Be?
Why Standeth Thou There?

...it read.

Then, the erstwhile charming prince entered the king's Great Hall, whereupon a courtier sidled up and whispered all in haste: "Dear prince, I beg of thee, forget me not when anon thou ascendeth the throne, for, I have always been loyal to thee in especial."

One after another, the smooth gentlemen of the court did privately pour their fealties into the prince's puzzled ear, 'til at last he stood a-dazed, wrapped in a brown study.

Then Jesper, with a merry caper, addressed the addled prince, *sotto voce*: "My Good Lord and my Liege, word hath run about like a bevy of kitchen mice that thou dost scheme and plot to crack the crowns of the king and Walter someday, and scramble us up a savory, new dish. 'Tis a feast we devoutly desire—save only that not too many eggs be broke in the makin' of it."

This and the like went on for three days more, until the prince said unto himself: "What ho! Am I not prince of this realm after all, and not some slothful cur asleep in the sun? Should I not stand at the head o' each and every palace intrigue? The World looks to a man to play his part, be he saint or Machiavel; and, a prince's subjects must regard their lord with love and awe, or else what a discord follows."

In a trice, the noble prince hiked up his silken hose and garters, brushed clean his velvet doublet and royal cloak of blue, powdered afresh his finest wig, and vigorously scrubbed his perfect teeth with a new-cut willow twig.

From that day forth, he deployed his wondrous charm upon his subjects the whole realm 'round. For, come the day his schemes were to mature, he well knew that he'd require their admiration and fealty.

Nor did Prince Charming ever pass the mirror outside the Princely Bedchambers *sans* pausing to adjust his wig or brush a mote of dust from his ruffed lace collar or straighten the seam of his royal hose or assay his brilliant smile. Or, for that matter, without pondering anew the obscure inscription graven thereon.

This wondrous transformation Princess Jewel beheld with a glad heart and a merry eye. And, despite the many sidewise winks and furtive fingers laid beside noses and secret stratagems that filled the prince's days (though no grand coup or heavy hand e'er struck at the king and his aging counselors), none complained. For was their prince not more handsome, more elegant and more charming than ever?

From time to time, Princess Jewel did cast a knowing glance at Jesper, the aping fool, who would then mime for her a diligent gardener at his toil or, sometime, a barnyard dog in hot and joyous pursuit of a rattling cart and horse.

Tale the Twentieth
Maddy and Her Gypsy King—A Rhyme

Young Maddy stands by her postern gate, where rude and narrow wends the lane to who knows why or where? As wary as a woodland hare, she waits upon what fate the shadowy track may bear.

A shepherd's lass is Maddy, wrapped in a herder's cloak. And with her shepherd's crook she tends the sheep her father keeps. Yet, ever and anon, she eyes the wand'ring lane and wonders at the secrets rare that 'round its bend must sleep.

Then comes a song, both low and trill, that loud and louder swells, 'til glade and field alike it fills. And, down the twisty lane there comes a Rover striding bold. His hair is black as is a raven's wing; his mein, both trim and proud. Crimson is the scarf he wears; his eyes are honey gold. A ring of silver from one ear; and on his hand, a jewel. That gem alone tells all who see (save this untutored child) a Gypsy King is he that rules all nations wild.

"Greetings, fair one," this Traveler says. "Fain would I share a word—if words thou hast to share. For, long have I a-roving been along this dreary track."

But naught dares Maddy say nor lift her eyes to his. Yet, stops he there, and waits he there upon the shepherd lass.

"Come 'way with me, my pretty one," this Rover whispers low. "And thou canst show me grove or down wherein we'll find good ease. For wild and free the winds do blow, and silver shines the moon. And as they do, so shalt we two, 'til midnight turns to light."

Poor Maddy then doth rise, as one within a dream, and leaves her father's gate, her father's flocks and fold, to seek the greenwood deep.

Nor speaks she yet; but in her breast, a wondrous fire there burns, with flame that neither wounds nor balms, the like she's never known. Nor thinks she of her father's care, nor of her brothers twain. The Traveler's words and Traveler's songs are all that she can hear.

Soon come they to a pleasant lea within the greenwood gloom, where all around the sweet birds sing and graze the white-tailed deer. 'Tis here fair Maddy sits her down and lifts her eyes to his. "What dost thou have to offer me?" asks she, her gaze as bright as stars.

The king doth stroke her locks of brown and fondles her soft cheek. Brave tales he whispers to her then of towns and countries far—such tales she's thrilled to hear. Thus, out he spreads his Rover's net—so wide it snares her sky. And, in a dream, her heart he warms and touches soft her thigh.

Throws she aside her shepherd's crook and casts away her weeds, and tup they there as ram and ewe amidst the greenwood leaves. Fast join they their hands; fast, too, join they their hearts. They dance and sing as lovers do, beneath the silver moon.

Apace dawn draws nigh and Maddy fearful cries: "Bide here, my Traveler true! Stay thou but here with me. Bairns five and three I'll give to thee, and all my father's flocks. Here shall be a bower green, wherein Contentment dwells."

"Ah, no," says he; "that tempts me not. Of such have I no need. The world is wide, its joys and all its wonders new now call me to away! Their siren call is what I heed, nor can I bide with thee.

"Yet, maid, do fly with me and be my loving bride, and we shall make the highway home and friend the antlered hind. And all we find, I'll give to thee, where'er we may be—in field or glen, in town or lea, Lord and Lady of that realm are we. But, hesitate til morning's light and thou shalt find me gone."

At this, young Maddy ponders deep. She 'visions far-off lands: the colors bright of silken gowns and mountains proud and steep. She thinks how road leads on to road, and lane turns into way; and of the Rovers that do roam, and of the love she has to give her daring Gypsy King.

Then, with a rueful sigh, her answer she doth make: "Each day, the tides do ebb and flow; each night, the moon doth sail. Yet, each returneth back again unto its proper place. Like them, good sir, must I.

"New lands and 'ventures strange must stay like distant dreams to me; for I was born a shepherd's lass and here my duty lies, where kith and kin and pastures green reward the humble heart. And sir, yon road is but a snare and leads one who knows where."

Then breaks that dawn; and flown has he, whilst Maddy waits behind.

The years do come and years do go, and o'er her children two, sweet Cuddie and wee Bonny Dee, dear Maddy keeps her watch. She watches o'er her husband, too, who slumbers deeply by.

Such times as these, in ember's glow, she sits alone and thinks: "Where be my Gypsy lover now, and where might I be, too, had his sweet song of living free once carried me away?"

While, in a darkling glen close by, there rests the Gypsy King. His eye falls on the sleeping host who journey with him now: his wives, all three, and children, too, a-slumber on the ground.

'Tis then, this king of road and mist and starry nights and all weighs what he gained and what he lost the time he strayed so far beyond a humble lass's love.

Tale the Twenty-first
Three Wise Men of Addleford

Once, in the very ordinary village of Addleford that
sleeps in the crook of Ninnysdale below the Great Scarf
near Folly's Crag, there appeared three pilgrims, each
robed in brown and shod in woven sandals of hemp.

One was swarthy and lean as a rake; the next was red
and round as a berry; the third peered at the peaceful
village with the squinting eyes of an unearthed mole. The
first two hailed this latter pilgrim as "Brother Eyesore,"
whilst he hailed them as "Brother Utterword" and
"Brother Toldhew."

Know ye that Addleford was drowsy indeed, where
nothing in living memory had chanc'd save that what had
hapt the day before. Where each villager went through life
with nary a thought in his head save what was for supper,
nor a word upon her lips save whether 'twas warmer this

day than yester or, mayhap, a titch colder. Where each took what comfort was to be found in the familiar round of wants and plans and toil.

It took Brother Eyesore no more than a blink of his moley eyes to take the measure of the place.

"Let us stop here a spell and refresh ourselves. For, I perceive that the folk here 'round be in need of our enlightenment and will welcome us in, once they learn the end and aim of our teachings," he announced.

"We three—as always—be of like mind; therefore, let us do so," chimed in both Brother Utterword and Brother Toldhew as one.

Thus saying, they strode o'er the splintered threshold of the Swan and Duck, wherein the Elders of Addleford sat, gnawing at their breakfasts of cider and crusts and cheese in the company of bored Friar Feather and good Mistress Flagon.

"Greetings, my good fellows," exclaimed that dame. "Be ye in want of food and drink? For, of that I have aplenty."

"Nay, nay," replied Brother Eyesore; "though thank thee do we kindly. Rather, we have come hence to offer ye something else—a boon that every man doth need."

"And what, pray tell, be that?" asked Elder Dunston, crust crumbs cascading from his lips.

"'Tis no less a thing than Wisdom," announced Brother Toldhew.

"The Secret to a Well-led Life," tossed in Brother Utterword.

"Good sirs," objected Friar Feather, "there be no need for such enlightenment here; all that man and woman need know lies in The Holy Book, from which I declaim at every Mass and Evensong, as well befits my station. Thy generosity doth ye credit, no-the-less," he threw in lest he give the three pilgrims offense.

"My good Man of God," Brother Eyesore swiftly answered, "ne'er would we three humble pilgrims contravene nor contradict that Good Book of which thou speaketh. Clearly, it lays out the pattern and pathway to Heaven, and all wouldst do well to heed thy—I mean, of course—*Its* teachings."

These smooth words did sooth Friar Feather, who nodded his satisfaction.

"Still, we must dwell here on this Earth a while, and during that while, we must opt for lives of good or ill— albeit for a short time in the great span of All Eternity. 'Tis for this brief moment in time and this little space on Earth that we offer up the Wisdom gained from our arduous journeys. In return, we ask nothing of ye, save, perhaps, a bit of shelter and some small sustenance to sustain us on our way..."

"A not unreasonable request," opined Elder Noddy, rousing from sleep long enough to speak. "What harm would come were we to hear these gentles out?"

Despite the flustered friar's fluttery objections, the Village Elders welcomed the three pilgrims to their table and bid Mistress Flagon bring 'em fresh ale, fine cheese and a fresh crust o' bread.

'Twas the next dewy dawn but one when the blear-eyed folk of Addleford gathered before cock-crow in the village square, and huddled there in front of the Three Wise Men like a limp field of oats recently quashed by hail.

"'Tis essential to thy well-being," began Brother Utterword, "that ye empty thy minds of the three Great

Evils that be cousins of the Seven Deadly Sins. For, as the sins do bar thy path to Heaven, so do these earthlier evils make a stile too severe for ye to scramble o'er or through and thereby enter Earthly Paradise."

Ignoring Friar Feather's feeble squawk of protest, Brother Toldhew took up the tale: "These be the three we shall learn to purge: Desires, Dreams and Destiny. With these three evils banished from thy heads and from thy lives, ye may recover the Bliss our Ancient Parents did forfeit in Eden."

"Why, this be naught but foul blasphemy," grumbled Friar Feather more loudly—though no one heeded him now.

"First then, mind ye follow me in some mind-altering exertions," commanded Brother Eyesore, and he folded forward with his arms adangle near to his toes. This, the drowsy village folk did attempt to imitate.

In an instant, the air was filled with a snapping and a popping like footfalls upon dead twigs in a dry forest or green kindling toss'd, higgledy-piggledy, upon a hungry fire. Hard upon its heels came cries and moans of pain that rang out like voices from the flames of Purgatory.

Yet, Brother Eyesore's mole eyes gazed serenely above the bent backs of the villagers. "Hold steady; hold it," coached he.

At last he smiled all sweetly and said. "Well-a-day. The Forw'rd Bend of Beneficence being done, let us now move on to the Breath of Paradise."

Soon were the Addleford village folk huffing and puffing, some like weary cart horses at the close of day and others like leathern bellows stoking a smithy's fire. This they did 'til the eyes of Widow Waddles rolled up into her head and she toppled backward into the sorry grasp of Poxy Cyril.

"Well done and goodly too!" enthused Brother Utterword, when all were red of face and afroth with spittle. "Now take ye but a turn or two 'round the fields in the Trot o' Tolerance, whilst we three pilgrims keep count of thy circuits 'neath this shady oak." And, off jogged the red-faced Addleford folk upon their miles-long trek.

So it went the morning long.

First, the Three Men of Wisdom did lecture the folk on the folly of wanting that which they could not gain, of planning for that which they could not foresee, and of toiling for that to which they were not entitled.

Next, the Three Wise Men had them bow and scrape and lift weighty stones above their heads and tote the portly Widow Waddles 'round the village square upon their backs and run hither and thither along the hillsides on their hobbling feet.

'Twas sooner rather than later that the cries and howls of the Addleford folk ebbed to whimpers and whines and then to naught but a gasping silence.

"See ye, my friends, how thy minds have now become empty vessels, with space now for Calm and Peace?" said Brother Eyesore with a satisfied smile. "'Tis but a foretaste of the feast that awaits, once ye be as babes—or e'en beasts of the field—that live for whate'er the moment might bring."

And so it went, morning and night and through the days thereafter, 'til the good villagers of Addleford—they that had once toiled like ants—began to question all their prior striving. 'Twas then they gave o'er the ways they had known to trod instead the rocky path of Wisdom the Three

Wise Men taught.

Thus, Cobbler Carl did trim mismatched soles for pairs of shoes, while his thoughts meandered through obscure lanes and o'ergrown byways in search of Truth. Thus, did Goodwife Grimsell pump with nary a care at her churn 'til all its cream had curdled well past butter, whilst she mused on the singing of the tit and the soaring of the swallow.

Thus, Shepherd Hamlin stood stock-still whilst he 'visioned a noble three-master crossing a wide, green sea. As he stood so transfixed by the there and then, his rudderless sheep trouped into Farmer Faddle's fields, feasting there on whate'er grain they failed to trample.

Nor minded Farmer Faddle a whit, for he was settled beside his rick in contemplation of the clouds that drifted in the April sky, wondering whither they went once they'd sailed o'er Folly Crag.

E'en the Village Elders sat unmoving and empty-headed beside their neglected pots of ale like the carved saints in a country church. And, Mistress Flagon did wipe the selfsame beaker time and time again as she daydreamed of old loves that had faded long ago.

"There now," concluded Brother Eyesore. "This village and all the good folk in it pay us heed and are well on their way to Lives of Wisdom. 'Tis much we have accomplished—though there be much as yet undone!"

"'Twould be a grievous error to abandon 'em now!" agreed Brother Utterword.

"In especial now that they, one and all, do pay us good heed and good sustenance!" emphasized Brother Toldhew.

Now, in sooth, 'twas not quite *all* those dwelling there that paid the price for Wisdom; the old hag who lived at the edge of the wood and wore her somber robes had heard these Men of Wisdom, yet heeded them not.

"Fie," thought she, "have I not had my fill of gurus and men of wisdom and the keepers of flames bright and dull in many times and climes? Their intent, at times, may be good; but they are oft misunderstood, most especial by themselves. Some Wisdom is too rich a feast for simple stomachs, I ween."

This concluding, the crone was quick about her plan. That same night, when the moon was lost to its waning, she climbed—though some swear she did fly—to the tiptop of the tallest tree in the forest and raised there a burning brand, far brighter than any star.

"Hush now," she whispered to that tree. "This will not take long, and I shall take leave of thy dear leaves and branches in a mere trice."

"'Tis no bother, Mother," rustled the tree (formerly known as Brilliant Ben). "I trust thou to take the greatest of care."

At that selfsame moment, the Three Wise Men reposed in the Swan and Duck, sharing a lamb stew and a foaming pitcher of cider before retiring, bellies full, to their pallets of down and their dreams of ease.

"Hark ye, look there!" exclaimed Brother Utterword, pointing to the bright, new star beaming in the heavens outside the inn's dingy window.

"I spy it, I do!" cried Brother Eyesore. "'Tis wondrous bright!"

"Surely, 'tis a sign unto us!" claimed Brother Toldhew. "What else could it be?"

"'Tis a good omen, for certain sure, one that we must rise and pursue," they all agreed. "Why else be we pilgrims? Our time's come round at last!"

Come the morn, Mistress Flagon found three empty pallets in her bedchambers, three pots of half-drunk cider in her snuggery, and a greasy stew, barely tasted, upon her board. The Three Men of Wisdom, howe'er, were nowhere to be found.

"Mayhap 'tis better they art gone," remarked Elder Dunston to his fellows that afternoon. "I, for one, be footsore and bone-weary, e'en if my mind be empty and at peace."

At his words, Elder Noddy and Elder Natternot nodded with vigor, though Elder Natternot immediately grabbed his twinging neck. "Mayhap 'twill improve our village, also," said they. "There's been a sorry drop off in those little duties that keep our ship o' state on an even keel, we fear."

"Well said, say I. What harm can come from living the life we were destined for?" reasoned Elder Dunston further. "What harm, in word or in deed?"

As lofty frigates (and small barks, too) drift like specters out of a dense fog and float to port, so did the dazed villagers of Addleford slowly come home to themselves again. Soon enough, they'd moored themselves once more to their old habits: wanting what they could not have, planning for what they could not foresee, and toiling for what reward no one could truly tell.

Tale the Twenty-second
Dexter, Our Good Physician

Not every village in those days could boast its own physician. Ours was yclept Dexter, and he had drunk deep of the philosophers of Padua and Milan. More, he had pondered soberly on the Ancients, both of Greece and of Rome, and he'd leafed diligently through the scrolls of Moorish sages. This, at least, he swore to.

Good was our fortune to have a healer the likes of Dexter; and oft the sick, the halt and the suffering from ours and all the hamlets 'round repaired unto his mean cot.

Within a lamplit room hard by the kirk yard, Dexter kept his tools and quaint devices. Blades there were of many sizes and drills with bits, both small and great. There were vises and clamps and leather-wrapped mallets and a broad, high table with drains and straps to spare.

Basins and buckets aplenty there were for catching our blood; and all along the wall there dwelt, in murky vials of glass or jars of stone, the leeches Dexter liberally applied for the good of we, his grateful patients.

Though Painless I Be Not, Yet Cured Of Me Shall Ye Be

...so read the signboard above our good physician's door.

Thence limped the freeholder Black John, who had let fall a great stone upon his foot.

"I canna stand 'pon it for long, nor may I till my land nor tend my herd," he lamented.

"Hmm," replied our wise physician. "I'll have a look." When he had looked and saw, he announced: "Well, my good man, I am afraid that foot must needs come off. For, as the wise do say: *better 'tis to lop the rotted limb than uproot the healthy tree.*"

Sighed Black John then a weary sigh and clapped a cloth tight o'er his mouth as Dexter set a-sawing.

Thence came Goodwife Sarah.

"My dear doctor Dexter," quoth she; "I suffer a grievous pain within my head, just here behind me left eyeball. Nor can I eat nor sleep nor joy in my draughts o' mead, so tedious painful it be."

"Hmm. 'Tis a common affliction in dames thy age, I fear," mused our good doctor. "For certain sure, a vile demon hath lodged itself within thy pate and we needs must vent him out, else henceforth relief nor pleasure shalt thou have."

Then bound the goodwife up her mouth so that her

howls disturbed not the kirk-yard sleepers as Dexter set a-drilling.

Stood pale, young Marcus in the good doctor's doorway.

"Good Dexter," sighed he, "By night I am without sleep for the thoughts of blithe maidens that will not let me rest. Nay, I lie awake all in a sweat 'til dawn. Canst thou not help me regain my sweet repose?"

"Hmm," pondered our doctor a short time. "The Ancients teach there's oft an imbalance within the humors of youths such as thou. I can and shall lance thy vexing blood and rid thee of these nighttime visitations."

So did the mild youth bind up his mouth 'gainst his cries, as the good physician lanced him deep and spilled his blood into the basins there 'round.

Appeared there then at the cottage door fair Juliet, a maid of just thirteen.

"Doctor," whispered she, "my time hath come, I ween, and painful it doth be. What canst thou do all privately to ease my maidenly distress?"

"Hmm," quoth Dexter. "This ailment doth stem from the moon and tides and from our wandering parents, Eve and Adam. I'll leech thee sore, as all the ancient philosophers proscribe."

Then, Dexter covered her milk-white arms and legs with a score of lusty leeches, while he nibbled on his luncheon fare of bread and cheese and ale.

Within our village and throughout the county wide did the fame of our good physician spread, and all around his handiwork was seen in the bloodless and limbless folk who trudged about in villages and on farms.

Yet our good Dexter was far from easy in his mind. No,

there lurked within his heart a shadowy fear that his cures did more harm than good.

"'Tis not possible to know," he mused, "had I but let Nature work Her Will, what may ha' befell. My art and craft and folk all demand that I act—and swiftly, too—and reck not the cost."

Dark grew the circles under good Dexter's eyes and ashy his wispy beard became. Murmured he unto himself each night as he sat alone in the Swan and Duck, swilling red wine and dark stout until the tapster closed the house.

"Something must be done ere our good physician a grave danger becometh," muttered our Village Elders at last. "But what could that thing be? Not wise nor learnèd enow are we to proffer counsel to such a physician as he."

Then, up piped young Jesper from his corner by the fire, where he rehearsed his apery of we villagers, one and all, saying: "Why, good nuncles, were I ye (though not I be), I wouldst send at once for the eld woman that dwelleth within the grim forest. For, though her fee be dear, oft doth she prove of good counsel, so say they all."

"Couldn't hurt," observed Elder Lewis with the rheumy eye. "Let us see what the old crone doth say." And, drained he his draught of ale.

In the gloaming of that same eve, a shadowy figure, stooped o'er a walking stick, appeared at Dexter's humble door.

"How may I avail thee, old woman," said our good physician, who was at that instant tapping a tun of cider.

"'Tis I, dear sir, that should ask that question of thee," replied this crone. "For, I am well paid to discover what ails thee, my good physician."

With much halting and circling about, Dexter at last

did ope the fears of his doubtful heart to that eld one. "Yet, I be still a man of science and practitioner of medical arts," he concluded; "one that hath delved deep into Hippocrates, Galen of Pergamon, Vesalius, Aristotle and all the more obscure ancients."

"Aye," replied she. "What thou sayest is true. Yet not every disquiet of body or mind requires mallet or drill or saw. Nor must every imbalance of bile or humor summon lancet or leech.

"Nature is sometimes like a bark upon the wind-toss'd seas. It rolls one way, then rocks t'other. And, that which She hath need of in such times is ballast, not a lighter load."

"I know not what thou meaneth," replied Dexter. "If an eye offends or a tooth pains, are we not commanded to pluck it out?"

"Nor is every ailment but a nail to be hammered down," parried the beldame. "Now and again, our craft cries out more for patience than for more force; at such times 'tis best to watch and be of solace."

Thus, the twain pondered and debated long, while the silver moon waxed and the owl and the fox stalked wee creatures in the night and the wind blew north to south and then to north again. Came the morn, both physician and his guest had fled, we knew not where.

Nor did he return that day nor the next. By week's end, we railed at our Village Elders: "'Tis a fine olio ye ha' served up! Now have we lost our good physician, and surely will we die of one fevered ague or t'other—and sooner not later, too."

The while, Jesper, that young imp, did jape and mime a sickness. Coughed he and spun he 'round and staggered he about until down he fell, his legs a-twitching in the air. "Be of good cheer, albeit I die," croaked that little clown.

But none of us laughed. The Village Elders filed into the Swan and Duck and called for three pots of the strongest ale.

At last, Dexter appeared once more in the physician's cot, and we all flocked unto his door, our drawn faces full of hope and pain. In we marched, like good physician's patients, and out we came with limbs intact and blood untapped and wonderment upon our selfsame faces. In but a day less than a fortnight, we villagers had gathered once again in the village square to raise our angry voices.

"Why, our doctor is but a fraud," quoth one, "a cheat and a charlatan."

"Aye! He told me that I must weigh two stones less were I to relieve these pains in my knees and back," complained Widow Waddles.

"Told me, he did, that I should leave my easeful seat next to the fire and exercise me legs and arms the more," moaned Lazy Lawrence. "A man of my age and dignity! Imagine!"

"And 'e ordered me to eat green, leafy things—and apples, too!"

"And commended to me less ale and more sleep."

"He sent me to seek out Molly, the barmaid," shyly 'fessed the youth with sleepless eyes.

"Gave he me a brew of tree bark and herbs and grasses to ease me monthlies," whispered a modest maiden. "What witch or wiccan or necromancer would do less?"

"And he gave unto me a bag of leaves and twigs withal to make a wholesome tea," croaked a wizened dame.

"He dared tell me there be no better physician than

mine own self for my aches," bellowed the publican. "What kind o' doctorin' call ye that?"

"Aye," shouted we all. "Who shalt rid us of this worthless quack? Where be yon Elders now?"

And so it came to pass that Dexter fled our village within the hour by the north lane that leads we know not where. As he passed, one and all did hurl after him our curses, ill-wishes and barnyard ordure.

Yet, our Elders, e'er good and wise, did insure that he left behind his keen physician's tools: the saws, the drills, the lancets and the knives, the bowls and basins, and the leeches live.

For, should a new doctor e'er settle here, he might take up those tools and deliver to us the treatments we so desire and so deserve.

Tale the Twenty-third
Came There a Gentle Knight Errant

"**Hold, hold!**" quoth the knight astride his spavin charger. "Speak more plainly, if thou canst."

Sighed the good knight's clever squire and repeated the riddle, this time more slowly:

"All that there exists is all there is," said this squire, "including, of course, that which is not. Which meaneth, *ergo*, what is not must yet also exist."

"Why, 'tis not possible," protested the knight. "For how canst that which is not be also that which is?"

"Do we not speak of that-what-is-not with the same breath as that-what-is?" rejoined his trusty squire. "Just so, white cannot be lest there be black to set it off; nor can there be the sunny face of a golden gilder save there be an obverse side as well."

The noble knight went ambling on, a-pondering atop

his drowsing steed. Sir Gerald was this brave knight yclept, and all rusted and dented was his armor, long exposed to rain and wind, blazing sun and icy cold. Long since had the feathered crest molted from his lofty helm; whilst the badger rearing rampant upon his shield had long since faded to a dim smudge within a dull, gilt pentangle o'er scribed with this obscure motto:

suppliciter quaeritis

A mere pace or twain behind, his loyal Squire D'Wayne trod through the dank forest, wrapped close in a dingy cloak of persimmon and grey. In his squire's pack, he bore naught but a hunk of cheese and a well-gnawed crust or two of bread; and his fustian squire's sack was all but empty. For nigh a fortnight, these two had wandered through this mazy wood in bootless quest of bold deed or maiden fair.

"That be as pointless as thy other riddle about the flowing river into which I may step time and again, yet 'tis ne'er the same river as afore. Thou doth bandy words about like shuttlecocks, I trow," grumbled Sir Gerald.

"True, Sire," admitted D'Wayne; "'tis kin to that puzzle, sure. Yet, 'tis not mine in birth nor in tellin'. Something to tickle one's pate with whilst we make our slow and weary way, that's all."

"Bah!" spat Sir Gerald, suddenly wroth. "These be but silly games that waste idle hours. I have half a mind to leave you here, friendless in this tiresome wood. What a wretched squire hast thou been to me, lo, these many years!"

"Take heed, Sire," replied the squire. "Rash words be

like hurled stones—once loosed, they canna be called back again." Nor did the ingenious squire observe aloud that neither he nor Sir Gerald did, in any case, know where they were or whence they were bound. That thought he kept unto himself.

A mere half league on, from a coppice more close and drear than any the squire and his knight had yet encountered, sprang two bold highwaymen.

"Deliver and stand ye fast!" shouted one in a voice like a bullfrog's.

"Thou idiot," hissed the other. "'Tis 'stand and deliver!' E'en a dolt knoweth that."

"Well, then, Good Wisdom; suppose you face 'em down whilst I repose 'neath yon spreading yew." And off the first brigand huffed.

"Forgive us, good sirs," continued the second highwayman. "I fear we have yet to perfect our trade. Natheless, I must needs insist upon the contents of thy bags, sacks and baggage there."

"Thou saucy knave," retorted Sir Gerald. "See thee not that I be wending homeward, like the sage Odysseus, from my sacred quest in the Great World, all wearied and sore and *sans* reward? Sad to tell, quests prove not so profitable in these times as erstwhile they did."

"Why then didst thou go forth in the first place?" queried the thief.

"Why, to put Apostacy and Confusion to the sword, of course," replied Sir Gerald. "And to display unto the world a Virtuous Knight and True."

"And didst thou?"

"Alas, when I arrived to the Caliphate, found I that the Saracen were doing the job much better than ever I could.

With dirk and scimitar and sword they were hotly at one another's throats. To speak more generally, I greatly fear the age of knights bold and true has come and gone, leaving but a few of my kind to contend 'gainst the evils of these shrunken times."

"Noticed that, we 'ave," observed the villain. "Why, 'tis a rare day in May should a damsel in distress deign pass this way. 'Tis naught but merchants and clergy and functionaries, save for the occasional herdsman or tinker—and your honorable self, to be sure. Here now. I forget meself. 'Stand and deliver,' say I, or there'll be the Devil to pay!"

At these threatening words, Sir Gerald did unsheathe his rusty blade and brandish it with vehemence above the highwayman's head. Whereat, forth from under yon spreading yew, the other villain did spring, a wadded and cocked blunderbuss in his trembling fist.

"Hold there!" exclaimed the good Squire D'Wayne. "Gentles, let us not be hasty. Though this noble knight hath nothing to show for his travails, yet welcome to his nothing ye art. Nothing begets nothing, 'tis said; and we beggarly travelers have a sure surfeit of nothing."

"What didst he just say, Dinkin?" asked he of the trembling blunderbuss.

"Oh, ne'er ye mind, thou dullard," hissed his fellow. "And, how oft must I tell thee, oafish Lesley, not to utter our names when we be in company?"

Then turned the highwayman Dinkin to Squire D'Wayne. "Well now. Spill it forth and we'll decide."

Upon the leaf-meal ground there in the dark grove, the loyal squire did lay out the meager fruits of Sir Gerald's noble quest: the crusts of dark bread, the moldy cheese, a rent map of places unnamed, an ancient lamp, a copper coin or twain, and all manner of twine and thread and piebald patches. Yet, the clever squire craftily concealed close within his breaches a leathern purse and its few remaining gold coins.

"'Tis a poor lot indeed," said Dinkin looking o'er the paltry haul. "But, we must all take our livings as we can."

Lesley did lay his weapon aside and snatch up the ancient lamp.

"Why, this be a worthless thing, surely," said he. "It hath nor wick nor oil to light the way." He buffed the brass lamp all vigorously upon his leathern sleeve. "Nor will it take a shine, no matter how I rub," complained that ruffian.

Then, with a clap of thunder, the dark wood was filled with a cloud of azure smoke so thick it obscured the path and all the wild undergrowth thereabout. The brigands two, the noble knight, his squire and the weary, white steed all set a-coughing and a-sneezing while their eyes bleared o'er with tears.

Out from this azure cloud leapt a djinn. Yellow-golden was the jeweled turban upon his vain head; pantaloons of the richest scarlet silk girded his powerful legs, and, circled about his narrow waist was a sash of forest green. From his wrists and from his ears dangled bangles of copper and silver, and his lapis-blue slippers were of the softest doeskin.

"O! How I do love that entrance," laughed this djinn, standing with arms akimbo before the gasping troupe. "'Tis much superior to a blare of trumpets or parade of virgins strewing fragrant petals at my feet!

"But, what have we here? Do I not know this place?

Have I not paced these deep woods afore? Nearby, there be a woman—now eld I ween—but fair and loving, lo, these many years gone. I must pay her a visit ere my work here is done. And, done it soon must be; for, the awe and wisdom that cometh from gnomic riddles and dusty lamps grab not the imagination as once they did, I fear."

The four men and one horse stood with mouths agape and eyes a-water as the marvelous djinn orated thus and the azure smoke wafted among the branches and brambles of the forest.

Then, the djinn addressed the robbers twain: "Lads, ye be wasting thy time with these poor, molting birds. I know for certain—do not ask how—that yonder rides the grasping Laird Clarendon with but a small and simpering retinue and pockets stuffed with the rents of his groaning tenants. Hie thee hence and waylay him; nor will any protest but he. Mind ye, lest ye see the likes of me again, return all unto the poor that he hath robbed save a shilling or two for thy labors. Watching you close, will I be!"

"That we shall do!" promised Dinkin and Lesley in haste, and off they scuttled.

"Well then: I shalt now address your situation, e'en though ye have not yet wished aloud, as the rules clearly stipulate. After which, I'll call upon that dear one who dwells within this forest. Doubtless she'll be o'erjoyed to see me." (So high was the self-regard of this glorious djinn.)

"Good Sir," mused he on, his be-ringed hand stroking his lustrous goatee, "here be thou, an earnest knight and true seeking adventure far and wide to test and prove thy mettle. Mayhap, the Age of Chivalry and Knights Errant hath waned (as have so many other good things of late);

yet, that meaneth not that thou must sink into boorishness or drink or into the rank and odorous Slough of Glum.

"How oft we seek abroad that which sits so near to home!" this most philosophical of djinns rambled on. "I am sure that much good couldst thou do wert thou to patrol this dangerous and deceitful wood, confounding its evils with thy acts of bold courage. Is it not better that thou shine in this good use than rust *sans* aim or purpose as thou dost now?

"And hark! Do I not hear I a maiden's distressed cries from just past yon stand of oak as I speak?" At this, the djinn put a jeweled hand unto his be-bangled ear, like a bad actor in a pathetic play.

As Squire D'Wayne gathered up in haste their few worldly goods, Sir Gerald did spur his charger into a wheezing trot. In a trice, the good knight came upon a beauteous maid, tresses of gold and skin of cream, chained roughly to a stout tree trunk, whilst a greedy lion circled her 'round, froth dripping from its terrible jaws.

Then forth did Sir Gerald's sword sing and off the lion shrewdly fled. The good knight touched the tip of his rusty blade to the chains that bound her fast, and those chains fell from that fair maiden, as light and silent as ribbons that drop from a milkmaid's cap on May Day.

With modest smile, the lovely maid did part her ruby lips, whence sprang a song of purest rapture. Before the knight and squire's amazèd eyes, she metamorphosed into a beauteous bird with wings of rainbow hue, that soared above the leafy maze and was gone, save for her echoing song.

And then, like new-fall'n snow falls from a wind-tossed bough, the rust did rain from Sir Gerald's sword and his dull armor. Bright gleamed his shield now. Plucking up a glorious plume that the maiden-bird had shed, he affixed it to the silver helm he wore upon his head. Sir Gerald's spavin steed now grew plump and sleek, and e'en the lowly squire's patched cloak and tattered cap were as newly bright as a June morning.

"Here in this vast forest shalt we abide henceforth, and here shalt we many more adventures seek," proclaimed that good knight boldly. "Here, at last, have I come upon the true heart and soul of my long quest. As the sage djinn did say: chivalry begins at home, and home is where we now be."

"Right thou art, Good Sire" responded his subtle squire. "For who wouldst thou be wert thou not who thou art?"

"Hold thy waggish tongue, Sirrah, and give me but a moment to parse thy twisty words," mulled Sir Gerald, trotting along briskly through dappled glen and shaded copse, his faithful squire once more but a pace or two arear.

Tale the Twenty-fourth
Ballad of the Faithful Soldier

Bright shone the sun, no cloud did mar the sky, as forth the stalwart soldiers strode. Of emerald were their tunics green; of scarlet was each sash. The polished brass upon each coat did blaze like fire and blue were all their banners.

Loud rang the trumpets then, and louder beat the drums. And louder still the townsfolk cheered, as from both hill and wood, their glad shouting did resound. And then, as dreams in morning light, those echoes died away, and all was just as if their cheers had ne'er been upraised.

From high upon his dappled steed, their proud Captain cried, "This day we march to glorious fray. Our sabers are of sharpest steel; our guns, well-armed with shot. When this day ends, our foe shalt lie before us prone, and, victorious, come we home!"

O'er wold and o'er the hills beyond, the valiant column coursed. Whilst o'er the town that urged them on, there fell a winter chill.

Long fair Dowlin lingered there, long since the troop had passed her by. And there, unto her soldier, Drew, she whispered this fierce vow:

> *Here wait I each night for thee, though foolish and old*
> *   I grow.*
> *For, thy caress and thy dear kiss mean more than life*
> *   to me.*

And from the hill not far away, her soldier dear the selfsame words did swear:

> *I pledge to thee my sound return, though fierce the foe*
> *   may be;*
> *And, though the battle rings me 'round, thy love shall*
> *   guide me home.*

For, Drew loved Dowlin as he loved life; and she loved him back the same. As leaf and blossom were those two; their love, the root and branch.

Before the April sun'd grown warm, the soldiers brave came unto a meadow green. Their chary Captain paused him there, once more to rouse his troops.

"My lads, be bold, and forward charge—for yon the cowards crouch. With cold hearts and colder steel, now roust them out, and, lo, the day is thine! Here will I stay— a way apart—with cannon primed and set. March on, my lads! March on, for fate's bright triumph waits!"

Across the meadow green, the eager soldiers charged.

Above, their pennants blue unfurled; below, their feet did fly. Their emerald column was an arrow loosed straight at the foe's dread breast, its fateful course was set.

And as he sped across that lea, Drew prayed unto himself that Dowlin's love might keep him safe throughout the clash to come.

Let wild and fierce this battle rage, thy love shall be my
 shield.
When all 'tis done, I shall return to home and hearth
 and thee.

Beside her postern gate, Dowlin stood waiting still. To quell her fear, a pledge she made and said it o'er again:

Here shall I wait 'til I am old, whate'er be thy fate.
For thy caress and love's sweet kiss mean more than
 life to me.

Behind their crafty barricade, the wolfish foe crouched low. They watch'd the valiant troop come on with narrowed eyes and faces carved of stone. Sharpened were their cruel pikes, and crueler their knives of steel; and cruelest of them all, their hearts, as hard and cold as ice.

Then, floundered that fair legion in a pit this foe had dug. Like doom, up rose those swarthy men and fell upon the band in green. The pennant blue did halt in doubt, as from the forest nearby, a gory cavalry burst forth on frothing steeds, its sabers ready drawn.

The thunder of this counter-charge rang loud throughout that vale. And, from the hill whereon he sat, the Captain gaped in awe. He saw his noble column writhe, a sapling in a storm. Down went its pennants blue, trampled in the mud. Down went his green-clad soldiers true, before their deadly foe.

He turned his cold grey eyes away, nor could he watch the more. And, ere the sun was halfway run, ere pennant bright and crimson sash, trumpet and brave drum had failed, away he rode, never to return.

At gloaming in the silent town, the villagers are hid, their windows all are shuttered tight, their doors all strongly bolted.

Throughout a long and weary night, file ghostly figures by. Empty are those spirits' eyes—and empty are their hearts. No one bears witness to their march, nor dares a word be said, as to the grave these specters file, in ranks and rows, all dead.

All in that town save Dowlin hide; she only waits to see. With eager gaze, she eyes each shape that shambles slowly by; each vacant face, she searches now with hope that will not die.

At last, comes one tall form. His emerald coat hath turned to dun; his sash is rent and mired. Up to her gate, this figure glides, as 'twere a twilight's mist, and in its hollow voice, this tattered specter speaks:

I swore, My Heart, that I'd return, though deadly raged the fight.
And here shall I each night come back, if only thou so please.

As ashes do, Drew's kisses fall on Dowlin's eager lips. As smoke are his embraces sweet, as he draws Dowlin in.

This promise then she makes that she will always meet

him there, whatever fate may bring:

> *Here shall I wait for thee each night, though I grow old*
>   *and frail.*
> *Thy spectral kisses and light embrace shall hold my*
>   *life in thrall.*

Tale the Twenty-fifth
The Little Flower of Content

One darkling eve not long ago, a robed figure stooped into the low hovel of the agèd crone who dwelt deep within the forest. Low burned her humble fire in the grate, as her dog snored before the meager flame and her watchful cat dozed there beside it with one gold eye yet ajar.

"Why, Father Felix! 'Tis a surprise to see thee here at this late hour—or at any hour for that matter," observed the old woman, without turning her gaze from the fitful fire, but setting aside her foolscap and quill, nonetheless.

"I be surprised to find me here myself," murmured the good Man of God. "Yet, I am at my wit's end, and I have heard—though in whispers and sacred confessions—that when all else fails, thy dark powers may help bring about a wonder."

"Speak on," said the crone, "but mark thou: my arts do

oft lead down unexpected lanes where ends not foreseen do wait. The power to see all that lies ahead lies beyond my ken, I fear. But, prithee, do say on."

Then the reluctant priest did spill forth the woeful tale of a hamlet harsh. Where suspicion and resentment had sprung up like weeds alongside a country lane in August.

Should it fall out that Widow Margaret sported a new bonnet, why, then would Dame Marjorie at once declare it the ugliest headdress that e'er adorned a female's skull.

Should Yeoman Brown's field sprout lush and green, why then would Farmer Dale's sheep, by mal chance, break loose from their cote and feast upon the farmer's new corn. Should Goodwife Gretchen's hens lay large, speckled eggs, within but a day would word spread that speckled eggs were foul rotten.

When tender Lassen did compose an ode to spring, did not the bully Jakes and rough Rafe make of it a mocking song so cruel the poor lad dare not show his face? When Maid Felicity accepted handsome Will'am as her suitor, did not the other village lasses claim that this very Will'am had lain with them, one and all, and moreover bore the pox?

"Not one bonny thing there is save that my petty flock shalt bring it low," the weary shepherd said of his sheep. "Nor can one neighbor rise lest another feel he hath fall'n. Each eyes his neighbor as a famished kestrel looks upon a meek coney in the grass below. I mayst as well be minister to beasts of prey, all ready to rend and tear; and I, alas, must list to each cruel confession, issue penance and promise mercy. Can we not just improve them, hearts and minds, instead?"

"I feel for thee," said the old woman after a moment's pause. "Nothing is harder than to dull the blade of Envy, nor anything less possible than to balance Jealousy's scales. Howe'er, there may be something we can try. What thinkest thou of this?

"There is a flower, blue as a maiden's eye, that grows secretly within this forest. 'Tis said that its pure nectar doth infuse the Milk of Kindness and Content into the breast of any that sips but a drop. I—and few others—know whereabouts it grows. Shall I fetch it hence for thee?"

"That, my dreary woman, may be the very elixir I need!" exclaimed Father Felix. "Bring me, I pray thee, but a few drops and I will slip 'em in the communion wine this very Friday."

"Done and done," said the old woman. "But mind thou one more time: neither thou nor I canst foresee whither this trial wends."

"I fear but a snipe hunt it be," observed the cat sourly, once the good Man of God had gone. "Oft thou hast said that women and men be what they be, no matter how we or they do strive for lasting change. Nay; 'twill end badly, I trow—though take I no pleasure from saying so." And, the cynical cat fell to licking a velvet paw.

"Still and all, I would not see that Man of Faith in such despair," countered the beldame. "Is it not better to strive, e'en against that which resists change more than a balky mule? Is it not the strife itself that makes a cause just? Mayhap, we ha' failed before; yet can we not hope for one new trick, e'en from an old dog?"

"What?" said the dog, stirring by the fire. "What dog be we talking of now?"

"Never mind thou," hissed the cat.

In the market square on a sun-bathed Saturday that followed, the hamlet folk did marvel. For, what they heard and saw there was the like of which they had ne'er heard nor seen before.

"Good morrow, Goodwife! Wondrous fine must be those hens o' thine, for the eggs they be a-layin' are large and fine as a roast o' beef!"

"How well them ribbons look, dear lady, upon thy brave new bonnet!"

"Ne'er have I seen sheep so wooly and so rotund as thine, my good man. Do tell: how dost thou wean them?"

"I 'spect thy corn shall reach the oxen's eyes ere the month is out. What be thy secret?"

"Heard I not that thy wealthy uncle did pass and leave thee all his fortune—that selfsame uncle thou hast ne'er known nor seen? Felicitations on thy good fortune, and come, let us buy thee a pot o' ale!"

"Couldst thou not, dear Lassen, compose one o' thy beauteous odes for Old Growler, me faithful hound?"

"Blithe are we all that sweet Will'am and thou hath one another found, and look we forward to thy wedding day."

This, and more of the same, the village folk heard echoing round the commons, as Father Felix stood by, out-beaming old Sol himself.

And so it went, day in and day out, for nigh unto a fortnight. 'Twas the most neighborly hamlet on this earth since Eden. In the confessional, Father Felix heard namore of hearts brimming o'er with Jealousy, Resentment and Envy...

...instead, his sullen flock did begin to complain of a whole new malady.

"I reck not that what ails me, Father; but, all seems pointless to me now."

"Well knowst I that I should be content—for, have I not

enough as doth my neighbor? But no rest do I find from the dark thought that someone, somewhere may yet ha' a little bit more."

"'Tis like I be swimming through muck and mire in a dream—all gallantly I strive, yet no progress I maketh."

"Hath I not all that a man could need? And, dwell I not amongst good and happy neighbors all 'round? Whence then, cometh this hollow feeling near my heart?"

"How stale and profitless this world doth seem, though all do sing my praises!"

Then, the good Father stood hip-deep in Perplexity and Doubt. At last, he tromped back through the forest drear unto the witch's low door. He found her again, seated beside a low fire a-scribbling on a folio of foolscap.

"Greetings, Right Reverend One," said she, not looking up. "Do I not hear that all goeth awry with thy fat and contented flock?"

"'Tis sad. 'Tis true," sighed this good Man of the Cloth. "For though all do greet and cheer one another like good neighbors aught, yet a malaise hath crept in like a lowland contagion. The more they praise and glorify their neighbors, the more do they feel a sickly, cold ague upon their troubled hearts."

"Ah, woe," sighed the old woman at his words. "'Twas worth a hazard, I thought. It 'pears our hopeful experiment hath run aground. 'Tis best we discontinue this treatment and return the patient back to his basil nature. 'Tis a poor physician of body or of soul that replaceth one ill with but another."

"I fear thou speaketh sooth," said the weary Father. "Namore elixir will I dispense, come what may. Yet, 'twas a noble experiment, was it not?"

"Aye; and are they not all?" replied the crone kindly. "Some blessèd day, one trial may fall out well, and, 'til that happy day, in confusion and failure we beat on."

As Father Felix made his way back through the dim forest, the old woman took up her pen and ink again and her dog and cat roused themselves from where they dozed.

"I trow nor husband nor goodwife can be content leastwise they see their good fortune reflected in the dark mirror of another's ill," mused the cat, coolly licking her paw.

"Why is it, I wonder, that woman and man hath such great, unfailing skill at finding the ill in their lives?" yawned the dog. "Mayhap 'tis on account o' those what-do-you-call-'ems they have upon their paws..."

"*Thumbs*," sighed the cat, "thou meaneth *thumbs*."

"Them's the very things," said the dog brightly. "Them *thumbs* be what makes 'em prone to grasp too high, e'en though they are like blind-born pups. Nay, this world be of odors o'erripe or fresh and breathe all of 'em in I do, *sans* question. For, what boots it to eye a gift too narrowly when a gift be laid afore thee?"

"Now seest I that e'en the dimmest day may have a ray of sunshine. Praise be, thou hast a point there," observed the cat loftily. "From what I've seen, humans be a-striving always to o'erturn their neighbors' good fortunes."

"But, my dears, the fault lies not in their deeds, but in their hearts," put in the old witch, scribbling away heroically. "Truly 'tis said: a pure heart is but an empty gourd and cannot long abide in this world. 'Tis our passions that make cool Content and green-eyed Jealousy, the Janus faces on the dear coin of our lives."

"Therefore, I am glad I follow but my nose,"

pronounced the dog.

"Indeed, thou art the most simple-minded creature," sniffed the cat.

Thus, their debate did flair and roll on all through that moonless night 'til a new day broke.

Tale the Twenty-sixth
The Princess and Her Suitors Three

Once, not so very long ago, there lived a princess as fair as is a summer's day. Like flame were her flowing tresses; her form, supple as a willow, and her bright eyes were as sapphires blue. Throughout her father's fiefdom, each and all did sing her praises, and she was courted by three bold and handsome suitors.

As is the way of things in such **Tales** as these, their curly locks were all honey blond o'er noble brows. Their chests were broad and their shoulders wide; their chins were cleft, and the light in their eyes danced like the sun on the teal-blue waves of the sea.

Equal were they in fortune, age and birth; and therefore, was the poor princess, though flattered by this embarrassment of worthy suitors, at great pains o'er which or how to choose 'mongst 'em.

"Dearest Mother," she appealed to the queen, "whate'er shall I do? Am I not the proverbial ass caught twixt two equally delectable bales of hay? He that's turned to stone in indecision? Yet, I must choose it seems, for all eyes be upon me, and my majority approaches like a thief in the night." At which, a crystal tear slid down the princess's unblemished cheek.

"There, there now," soothed the kindly queen. "Thou wert, in sooth, born a Child of Fortune, as 'twas foretold at thy cradle side. Therefore, not many a maid hath either your chance nor your choice. Well I ken that good fortune hath its burdens. Bethinketh me now how 'twas when I had to opt twixt your father—our noble king, God-bless-'im—and that rich merchant's son with the pearl-white teeth, artful song and shapely calf.

"Tut, my child. Put but an end to all this sighing and calf's-eyeing! I'll send for the old woman who dwells deep within the dark forest, for 'twas she that counseled me in my time of confusion and shall, no doubt, assist thee in thine, as well," comforted the queen, brushing away the princess's crystal tear.

That very eve, as a silver sliver of moon slid behind a murky cloud and a hush fell o'er the night fowl, a shadowy figure did steal into the Princess's Bedchamber, wherein awaited the queen and her fair but trembling daughter.

"'Tis good to see thee again, dear Madam," said this witch. "All's well as goes well, I trust."

"Well enow with me," replied the queen. "But alas, it goes ill with my daughter, the princess, here. For she is in a poor maid's quandary and in sore need of help to select her a husband."

"Ah, I see," said the crone, eyeing the cringing princess

narrowly. "Husbands do be difficult to choose—and then to manage—I well know. Goodness! My share of 'em I've seen, for certain. Be thee not afeard, My Pretty, for help and succor I am here to provide."

The old woman then took the princess's dainty chin in her gnarled fingers and gazed into her chalk-white face. "Three there be, I perceive," said she after a moment's inspection, "and they be rather hard to tell apart, it seems. This be a fine kettle o' fish, for thou must decide with which of 'em to spend thy happily-ever-afters. Well now, rest thou easy for I have a plan."

"Do tell," urged the queen.

"I propose but this: to spend one night each with these handsome and bold suitors, masquerading as this fair beauty here, and, by the third morrow, I shall give thee measures tried and true as to which the best husband for thee shall be."

"But sure as sunrise, they shalt see thou art not I!" sputtered the princess, eyeing the hag's humped form, wiry hair and wrinkled skin.

"Be not anxious on that point," simpered that old Amazon with a coy smile, "for, have I not craft and magic enow? That aside, young men, when they be about to spend a night in the company of their belovèds, do not oft, in my experience, peer too closely at the mare they've been gifted."

By these, and like arguments assuring the preservation of her dignity and her honor, the princess was quieted; and the queen and the witch set their gin in motion the very next night but two.

As midnight struck, the first suitor was ushered secretly into the Princess's Bedchamber, where veiled and perfumed awaited a gracious form. Passionate as the tides was this suitor, and the dark hours flew by in wild abandonment and sighs and cries.

"Too old for this am I getting," sighed the crone wearily as this first suitor crept out ere dawn's rosy light.

On the second night, came suitor the second, and he was gamesome and light, full of jibes and gossip of the court and town. In laughter and in jest, with foreheads pressed close together, did these two make the tedious hours run.

On the third night, appeared the final suitor with a kerchief stained by tears in his manly hand. Ere the first light of dawn, he had poured forth all the secrets of his heart, its dark fears and fond dreams, as water is poured forth upon sere ground. Then laid he his curly brow upon the fake princess's heaving breast and list with sympathetic ear like no other to her all hastily contrived thoughts, dreams and fears.

Upon his departure, did the old crone sigh wearily unto herself, "Too old, as well, for all that sharing am I getting."

On the fourth night, the eld crone crept back into the Princess's Bedchamber, wherein paced the queen and her anxious daughter. "What intelligence hast thou gleaned?" asked the queen. "Speak up quickly, for my daughter is nigh to death from anxiety."

"Thy choice, dear girl, 'tis plain as the wart upon my nose," observed the crone. "If thou wouldst spend thy days in perfect mutual understanding, why then the third suitor be the he for thee. Shouldst thou yearn, instead, for passionate love *sans* respite, why then choose suitor number one. Howe'er, if 'tis a boon companion—like e'en unto a brother—thou doth wish, one to laugh with o'er the foibles and follies o' the world, why bachelor number two is the best boy for thee."

Thereat sighed the princess all downcast: "High were my hopes of thee, old woman; yet now I fear thy arts be much o'er rated. Shall I not want each and all of those things in a husband, be he prince or common as the clay? Alas, here betwixt two—or rather three—bales of hay stand I still. . ."

Then the fairest of the fair sat down upon the cold marble floor of her chamber with her perfect mouth in a pretty pout and her eyes a-brimming like a baptismal font with tears as clear as glass.

"This will never do," protested the queen. "Seest thou not what thy counsel hath wrought? Naught but more confusion and misery."

"Aye, 'tis the cruelty of the World and stale Custom that forceth we poor maids to make such choices, whereas we would rather take 'em all and be done with it," sighed the old woman thoughtfully. "Yet, mayhap there is something we could attempt, if thou and yon lass do agree."

The three put their heads together and whispered there but for a minute or twain. After which, the witch concluded thus: "Above all else, my girl, be most certain to pose the question exactly as we ha' coined it here—for knowst thee well, such magic as mine works only when it be coincident with the deep inclinations of those it would work upon."

"So I shall," said the hopeful princess. "Just as thou dost instruct."

That very day but one, were the three exceedingly

perfect suitors summoned to the palace yard, wherein the princess waited. There, she asked each what he would vow to win her hand and heart fore'er.

"I should adore thee all the days of thy life and beyond," swore the first suitor, passion aflame in his teal-blue eyes.

"I should bring thee joy and laughter to lighten all thy days and illumine thy darkest nights, e'en to the end of time," said the second suitor, with a fraternal smile bright as the noonday sun.

Said the third with an earnest mien: "With me at thy beauteous side, ne'er shalt thou for a moment doubt my constancy nor deep intent, for I shall ope my troubled heart and mind unto thee freely all the days of our lives."

Then, the happy princess whispered into each suitor's perfect ear the exact words the old woman had taught her. Each suitor paused and looked askance at his fellows afore replying: "Yeah, e'en that will I undertake if such be thy desire." At which, the princess's smile was like Old Sol arising from his dewy bed upon a morn in May.

At the wedding of the princess, the bells did carol their triumphant song and the people of the fiefdom did raise their loud "huzzahs."

Yet, aside they asked one of the other: "Which one is the he that she hath chosen?"

"I canna tell, truth to say," was the common answer. "For, so far as I ken, the three were so like unto a pod o' peas that she shall be as content with the one as with t'other." So, turned they with no further ado to the ale and sweet delights the king and queen had lavished before them in celebration of their daughter's wedding.

And, from that day forth the princess did live in perfect

happiness.

Each day at dawn, she unlocked an hoary wardrobe sitting in her bedchamber, using the silver key that she and she alone did keep upon a silken thread about her neck. Upon three hooks within that upright chest there hung three shadows, each one grey as smoke.

Then did the princess whisper to herself: "Which husband shall be mine this day? What be the mood I'm in?"

...as she took one or the other of the shadows off its hook and breathed life into its willing lips.

Tale the Twenty-seventh
Amor Vincit

Hard by the sea strand, where reef and rock and tow'ring cliff make the briny waters churn, dwelt five fishers and their families in cots low-sheltered 'gainst the wind. There, they cast forth their nets when tides were high, and there they kept watch, both night and day, for sailing ships to pass them by.

Like swans, those lofty ships sailed by. Like clouds, their sails billowed. Their holds were laden with wealth from Africa, the Orient, the Netherlands and Spain. Yet, those proud ships dared not sail near the waters of Dead Fisher's Cove, where the fisher families dwelt.

Though poor they seemed, those families hid their treasure well, secreted in caves below the rugged cliffs. For, e'er and anon, a rich vessel would founder and fail amid the shoals, and then the tide would bring its goods and wealth ashore. Caskets of gold and jewels, tuns of choice wine and ale, fine silks, ingenious embroideries and fine china waited on the strand for the five fishers and their families to harvest in.

Amidst these five—but set a bit apart—lived Emmie, a fisher lass of but thirteen. For five years and more, she had dwelt alone, with only the sound of the sea in her ears and only the ocean wide to feast her eyes upon. Little said Emmie as she paced the stony strand, watching the grand ships that plied the rolling sea.

"What can love do?" she asked the heedless winds and waters. "No one have I to ease my heart or help me pass these empty hours. Who would love a lass such as I, who dwells apart on this bare strand?"

Then came a booming storm, its waves high as the forest trees and its winds roaring like that forest's ferocious beasts. Through this riot, drove the *Maria de Ouro*, a proud merchant from Lisbon, running before the awful blast with her lanterns all ablaze.

Suddenly, the *Maria* did strike the bar; and, with a moan that echoed 'round the cove, that brave vessel went down; and all her treasures rare, her captain and her crew, surrendered to the foaming brine.

Came the light before the dawn, and all the fishers and their kin were hard upon the strand, plucking up the wrack and ruin the pitiless sea had sent. Like carrion birds, they hovered in the early light, dark figures on the sand; and with them—but a space apart—did Emmie, too, the fisher's orphan, scavenge for her living.

She rummaged there 'midst rock and tidal pool, until she found the *Maria's* cabin boy. His beardless cheek and pale hands lay turned up to the sky.

Gone was his shoe, his stockings loosed about his shins, and his alabaster breast was bared. Empty were his milky eyes, wherein Emmie saw nothing but the boundless sea. Pure as snow was his brow, and his fine, young lips were blue.

On his slender finger gleamed a golden signet ring on which was artfully 'graved *"Meu Amor."* This trophy Emmie plucked in secret from his still finger and in haste placed it on her own. And, all the while his sightless gaze held her fast in thrall.

As the sun arose from the roiling sea, there issued from the boy's pale breast a gasp, between a groan and sigh, that cried out, *Emmeline.*

At the first light, the fishers five and their families hurried to their hidden caves around their treacherous cove. There they stowed their pelf with care and cast the dross back into the sea—the sad remains of the *Maria de Ouro*, the naked bodies of her crew, and among them, too, the cabin boy, a corpse more beautiful than all the rest.

For a fortnight's slumbers thereafter, Emmie lay upon her mat within her father's mean shelter. There in the darkness, the cabin boy's ring glowed upon her finger. *Meu Amor* it gleamed; and the beautiful cabin boy, too, whispered *amo-te muito* into her fitful dreams.

"Fear I for our dear Emmeline," said a fisher's wife one day, pulling the silver buckles off the satin slippers of the ship's proud captain. "She grows more pale and wild with ev'ry passing tide."

"Aye, 'tis so," replied the other, plucking brass buttons from a seaman's waistcoat. "'Tis five years and a day since her father rowed him out to sea, ne'er to be seen namore. Lone and watchful hath our girl been time since."

"I bring her oaten cakes and cider to ease her solitude," replied the other; "yet barely a single *tak* she utters, poor child."

"It be a pity that her mother lies long buried high upon the cliffs, for mothers are great comfort to young maids at such times as these. Come 'morrow and I shall bring her salt cod and apples twain."

And settled they back to their candled work, deep within a cave beyond the reach of the hungry waves.

For nigh unto a fortnight, amid the sounds of surf and gulls, the soft voice of the cabin boy came whispering like the wind*: Emmeline. Emmeline. Meu amor. Tu és bonita, meu amor*. And, in her dreams, both night and day, she thrilled to his embrace.

"Come with me, my own love and true," his sweet ghost wooed. "Come away and be my bride." The more that boy let Emmie neither rest nor eat, the more her heart grew wild and more distant grew her gaze. While, on her finger, his signet ring did pulse and burn as with a living fire.

At last cried she, "This can I bear no longer. That beauteous boy doth haunt me day and night; nor will he let me be—and I, alone in this wide world with mother dear nor father stern to guide me or advise."

Then, she kissed her father's lintel and closed his rough door tight. By the waning light of a wan moon, Emmie walked down to the sea.

Into the salt waters she waded 'til they closed above her head, and at a rocky shoal she waited, daring no breath to draw.

All at once the cabin boy swam up from the deep and he circled Emmie round.

"I see I've won thee now, my darling Emmeline," he smiled. "Here, 'neath these waters, we shall dwell henceforth, locked in fond embrace, so long as moons do rise and tides do run!"

Then, into her willing arms he swam and kissed her long and deep. Like ice were his lips and yet, they warmed her, heart and head. His eyes of pearl so stirred her soul that she neither struggled nor fled.

But, speak she did to say just this: "What can love not do now?"

Deep into the ocean's floor, her toes then delved, and there they anchored fast. Above her the restless waves tossed, while all below was calm. Anon, her tresses turned to green and coral spread down her arms; and there the gentlest creatures in the sea found refuge and repose.

In that strange time long ago, the waves in Emmie's Cove grew tame, and the waters there grew deep. And since that time, no opulent galleon or merchant brave did ever fail, nor sailors' lives nor treasures yield up themselves to canny fisher folk.

Amor vincit omnia, so all the poets hymn.

Tale the Twenty-eighth
The Founts of Wisdom

"**Restrain thyself, I prithee!**" hissed the cat, who was well fed and kept safe by the agèd crone that dwelt within the dark, drear forest. "Are we not now well out of sight of herself and the cottage window?"

"Forgive me, I pray," responded this same witch's dog; "for, seldom do we rove so far afield, and I forget meself when we get to roam this wood."

"Thou art a simple creature indeed," the cat sighed. "How I do wish that she wouldst not thrust us forth into the Great Wood on fool's errands. 'Tis but a thin excuse, I ween, to be rid of us for the day."

"But why would she that do?" asked the dog all pained. "Are we not her boon and only familiars?"

No sooner had the dog whined his question then there was a flash like lightening and a roar like that of a thousand lions from the dim glade where the eld woman's cottage nestled. Thence soon arose an azure smoke so thick it blotted out the weak sun that had but recently pierced the forest gloom.

"Hast thou now thy answer?" snorted the cat, blandly licking her velvet paw as the bright blue smoke drifted by. "There be naught for us to do, I fear, but tarry here 'til dusk. 'Twas a bold miscalculation—indeed, one o' her grandest—and I ween 'twill take the dear old thing the better part of the day to repair the damage done."

Discoursing thus betwixt themselves, the dog and cat paced further into the dark forest, the dog sniffing and grunting with delight and the cat grumbling as she followed along behind.

"What ho!" then exclaimed the dog, nosing over a flat, round stone. "What have we here?"

"Please be so kind, kind sir, and upright me, if thou canst; for, I have far yet to go in the name of Love," said the stone in a most lugubrious voice.

Back leapt the dog and uttered a sharp *yawp*.

"'Tis but a tortoise, innut?" observed the cat contemptuously. Then, to the tortoise she said, as she set it upright with her paw: "Why and wherefore?"

"Thankee kindly," replied the tortoise. "'Tis o'er yon brook and through the lea beyond that I be bound; for, there awaits Louisa, my heart's desire and my long life's love."

"Be thou nearly there, then," observed the dog.

"Another day or twain, in sooth, 'til our blissful reunion!" enthused the tortoise. "Natheless, ye canna hurry love, so they say; it hath its own pace and rhythm. She and I shall just have to wait, and therefore best I get on."

Then, the tortoise did 'gin to shift his ponderous legs and make his determined way, the light of love a-shining in his determined eyes.

As the dog and cat watched his laborious progress, there came a crashing in the bracken, and forth burst a roe deer, as fair and proud as e'er they'd seen.

Soft russet was her hide; wild excitement shone from her large, dark eyes, and from her dainty antlers streamed a crimson kerchief of silk.

"All must love me madly to pursue me so exceedingly," panted this elegant animal, as the baying of a dozen hounds or more sounded close nearby. "The chase is on once more!" cried she, and she leapt forth from that glade.

The dog and the cat were gawping still when, of a sudden, the cat crouched low and placed one deadly paw with deliberate care ahead of t'other. For, within but a king's reach, there was a small, brown sparrow rooting vigorously among the leaf meal that blanketed the forest floor. Yellow and burning bright were the cat's eyes, as closer and closer she crept to that hapless fowl.

"I wouldna try that, were I thou," said the bird, without looking round. "There may be consequences."

Paused the cat in her stalking and blinked her golden eyes. "What! Dare thou to threaten me, thy Pending Doom and thy Destruction?"

"I observe merely that, be we small or great, our actions have tails that follow upon 'em, no matter where they fly or what they be.

"Consider, *par exemple*, me," continued the tiny bird. "Though I be but small, have I not a place within the Grand Scheme o' Things? Here am I, busy gleaning and redistributing seeds about the forest floor. Were it not for me and my poor kith, would this pleasant glen not become o'ergrown with vine and bramble and contentious saplings? Who gainsays that I be essential to the health of this tangled place ye two calleth *home*? But, hurry-scurry— about my business I must go."

"Pah!" spat the cat. "This be naught but idle sophistry, and I'll ha' none of it." But, in the time it took her to utter these haughty words, the philosophical fowl had flown.

"Ho, ha," laughed the dog. "I do believe that 'un there got the better o' thee."

"Hush, thou simplest of beasts," muttered the cat. "Ne'er had I intention nor desire to prey upon her! 'Tis well known that such birds be but sour fruit, once ye get past all the feathers and scruff...But, hark! What noise heareth I now?"

Through the dim forest, there came a stout woodcutter and his buxom wife wreathed in dreary sorrow. They peered all about in the gloom and cried out with loud voices for their belovèd children, who had run off to spite their father and his new bride.

"Sore do I hope they find those two youngsters anon," quoth the dog, as the anxious couple passed them by. "Else shall the whole village be baying for our mistress's blood."

No sooner had he finished this sentiment, then a red vixen, with green eyes glancing warily all about her, slunk out of the brush.

"Dear Mistress Fox," said the cat, "Why so long of face? What afflicts thee, pray?"

"'Tis a kindness of thee to inquire," replied the wary fox. "But, not long may I tarry here, for they do hunt me with neither mercy nor respite."

"And why, prithee?" inquired the dog.

"Do they not pursue me for their sport? As flies to idle boys are we, mere toys to wile away a tedious afternoon. And yet, they begrudge my sweet kits and me a single fat hen or random goose—the very things they be saving for their own, groaning tables come the next high holiday. Where's the justice in that, I ask ye? Where be their sense of fair play?"

"Verily, it doth seem a trifle ill-balanced," admitted the dog. "Nor had I thought on it that way afore."

"Unfair and wearying, too," said the nervous animal. "It takes all my cunning and all my art to evade 'em. But hark! Hear ye not them baying hounds? I must fly, yet I leave ye with this riddle in thanks for thy kind audience:

What shineth like diamond, yet be black as pitch?"

And away dashed Mistress Fox.

Anon, through the brambles and leaves of a coppice, the dog and cat espied a plump, bejeweled noble born aloft in a gilded chair, gorging upon candied fruits and sweetmeats whilst his carriers trudged on.

"Deliver and stand," roared a voice.

"Dunderhead," roared a second. "How oft must I tell thee: 'tis *stand* first, and *deliver* thereafter!"

"Leave us move on," said the cat, "for, I fear these brigands mean harm to yon sticky-fingered lord."

In but a few steps further, came they then upon a mighty lion, asprawl in the grass. As the twain attempted to slip by unnoticed, the lion reared its noble head.

"No need to tiptoe, my friends," said the mighty beast mournfully. "I'll not attack thee."

"Whysoe'er not?" asked the cat, edging a bit further away from the lion's tawny paws despite his promise.

"What be the point?" explained the lion in a sorrowful voice. "Though I be the most terrible beast in the forest, what boots it? I have the most fearsome claws and eyes that pierce the gloom and teeth that rend like sabers. Yet, there be those that do challenge me here in mine very own realm and wouldst slay me with cold steel, given a chance. Woe and alack. 'Tis not that to which I was born, I ween."

As the two meanderers contemplated this melancholy king, they heard a jingling and a clanging approaching through the trees.

"Ah; pat on cue," said the lion mournfully, heaving himself to his feet. "They come, and flee I must, once more. With ye I leave merely my dignity."

With a great bound, the lion was over the hedge and across the narrow lane, down which pricked an armor-clad knight, a many-hued feather all radiant upon his proud crest, his shield and sword eager and at the ready.

"Good sir, do proceed a bit more slowly," wheezed his loyal and agèd squire, who limped along behind. "How will it fadge if our epic gest we attempt to tell all asweat and out-of-breath?"

This said, the knight and his complaining squire did vanish swiftly from the twain's sight, and the dog began to snuffle about the ground. "What have we here?" sniffed he, and he fell a-digging with his sharp nails.

"Hold, good sir, I pray thee; cease the action of thy heedless claws!" cried the little grey mole the dog dug out. "Well I knowst that thou could finish me off in but a trice, hadst thou a mind to. Yet, give me but a moment to smooth my fur and shield mine eyes from this glare..."

"I could snap thee in twain with but one bite o' my jaws," observed the dog grandly. "Give me one good reason I shouldn't."

"As thou seest, I be but among the slowest and the weakest of beasts, nor can I put up much of a fight, should thou desire one. 'Twould be o'er in a moment of terror and screaming. And then, where would the honor, the glory, or e'en the pleasure be in crushing so hapless a creature as I, one that offers to do thee no harm?

"From what little I can see," reasoned the nearly blind mole further, "thou seemeth sleek and well-fed to me, as doth thy companion there. So, need nor privation canst thou claim. To say more, while it be in the nature of things that the Weak fall prey to the Strong, 'tis incumbent upon the Strong, is it not, to exercise restraint and demonstrate compassion rather than raw power, wouldst thou not say?

"Though I be dim of sight nor spend much time out and about in the Great Wood, 'tis clear as day to me that the burden be greater upon those who have the greater power, and that, in the long run, 'twill be better for all if Consideration were the General Rule. Least ways, that is how it 'pears to me," the squinting animal concluded.

"Quite the social philosopher thou art," yawned the cat, who was getting weary of all their adventures. "Let us see what Master Dog hath to say in argument to the contrary."

"What? Wait. Could thou but repeat that?" said the befuddled dog. "For, I be thinking still about the riddle the wily fox put to us."

In this confusion, the mole stealthily tunneled back into the soft, rich earth that was his home and sanctuary.

Our two adventurers then paced on into a stand of tall and ancient trees, wherein the dog and cat observed a noble king and queen and their court retinue calling in vain for their beautiful and belovèd lost prince. From high amidst the leaves and branches, there came a constant whisper, as of voices conversing one with another, whilst the forlorn and anxious court passed by below.

"Oh, I like not this place," whined the dog. "There be a feeling here that maketh my heart's blood run cold and mine eyes see what I know is not there."

"Be not so foolish," said the cat. But she, too, gazed suspiciously about her with her great, golden eyes.

Hastily the two travelers retraced their courses, swift and true as thought, back to the dim glen wherein sat the old woman's cottage. All newly painted and appointed it was, with sparkling panes of window glass, fresh thatch upon the roof and bright, green ivy twining o'er the stone lintel. Therein, the weary dog and cat settled themselves before a modest hearth fire.

"Well, my dears, an' tell me true: what hast thou gleaned out there in the Great Wood this day?" asked the crone, a wisp of azure smoke yet wafting from her stray locks.

"'Tis naught but a dumb-show of noise and scurry," spat the sardonic cat; "signifying little. All do go about, absorbed in their own business, purblind as bats at noon. There's much more wisdom to be gained here by thy cozy fireside with thee, dear mistress," she concluded cloyingly.

Wide the footsore dog yawned ere adding: "For my part, there was much to see and smell and much of interest to greet my nose, had I but the wit and time to study on't more. Yet, I be drowsy now—and so shall I sleep, perchance to speak more of it on the morrow."

"Oh, what a simple creature thou art," hissed the cat, giving her tail a vicious lick.

"Thou art both true founts of wisdom," smiled the old woman. "Hush now, my dearies and rest—and by-the-by, the answer to the vixen's riddle is...

...*A Lie.*"

"A what?" exclaimed the dog. "Say that once more, I prithee, for I didna grasp it aright I fear."

Out came the witch's pen and paper then, as the cat sighed dramatically and curled herself up to sleep, nose under tail, hoping to dream.

Tale the Twenty-ninth
Burn the Witch—or Drown Her

"**But stay;** how shalt we fetch her here?" posed Elder Thomas, scratching his bald pate. "Be she a witch, as ye aver, wilt she turn not her Black Arts upon us 'n change me to a toad—or worse, a newt or a stone?"

"Bah!" snorted Widow Simms. "Thou art but a feckless cock e'en now, a-cluck-cluck-clucking all 'round the barnyard hens wi' naught to show for't. Woe to any village cursed with gutless fellows such as thou."

"Here now," piped up Elder Barnes. "'Tis ill to catch and bite amongst ourselves. We all want to see Justice inflicted upon the head of the evildoer. 'Tis but a question of how and when it may be done."

"No doubt there be but that she is a witch," shouted Goodwife Dulthea. "Of that let there be no more discussion, for the longer we shilly-shally, the more our dear daughters and handsome sons be drawn into her wily net."

"That be still to prove, I trow," offered Elder Winston, his triple chins atremble. "'Tis the point, after all, of hauling her afore Magistrate Mickle. Once 'tis determined she be a witch, the penalty's plain as the wart upon her nose."

"Doth she not dwell alone in the wood without any harm comin' to her?" shouted one.

"Doth she not dress in gloomy robes and roam the night when the moon is young, plucking up herbs and God-knows-what-all in the darkness?" protested another.

"Aye! And have I not heard her a-speaking to that cat and dog o' hers?" insisted a third.

"Once, when lost were we in the forest," said the woodcutter's fair boy, "did she not try to carve us up and roast us alive?"

"And stick us in a pasty-pie and eat us all up, too?" stoutly averred his straw-blond sister.

"In sooth, folk here-round have vanished mysteriously or turned to stone or mirrors or mounds of dirt whene'er she's been nigh," admitted Brother Dwindle. "I say this in all reluctance, as I abhor gossip, e'en about the Devil."

"She hath perverted our good surgeon," cried many villagers.

"She harbors brigands and villains in that forest o' hers 'til not one of us dares pass nigh to her dwelling," shouted others.

"My dear Bess stopped producin' not a fortnight after that eld one did swan by," insisted Farmer Sven in a loud voice.

"And who, then, might this Bess be?" queried Elder

Winston.

"None but me very best milch kine these fourteen year 'n more," said Sven stolidly. "Any but a fool knows that."

"'Tis but an old cow, then," muttered the elder, but none heard him, for, louder still had the outraged calls grown, within and without the Swan and Duck, to drive the witch out and, in that manner, rid the village of Evil.

Pondered they more the Elders did, though not long nor deep; for, they were schooled in village ways and could clearly see which way the tide did flow.

"Remains it yet for some one of us to go and fetch her here, where she shall stand trial and be condemned," pronounced Elder Barnes. "Be there any volunteers?"

"Gladly will I lend any good man and true my coney-catching snare," said Woodsman William.

"Alack, I have something that I must needs tend to, else I'd gladly go with 'em," said one.

"So, alas, have I," claimed one after another, 'til no one was left but a lad of six, who waved his wooden sword above his wee head and sang: *Hey-ho, the witch is dead—or slay her now I shall.*

"Men be but tubs of butter when there's summut to be done," snorted the Widow Simms. "Lots o' churnin' for a little thing that turns all soft in the light o' the sun! Wouldst ye have a thing be done, why, ask a goodwife, say I. Now, who's with me?"

In a trice, she snatched up the woodsman's coney net, and, in company of half a dozen goodwives more, marched resolutely off toward the witch's weird wood.

Not sixty paces beyond the village bridge, did those seven stout women come upon the agèd crone herself, dozing in the sun, her stick of polished yew wood leaning

’gainst the stone wall of a crumbling sheep cote.

"Seeking someone be ye?" quoth the eld one, bestirring herself. "And I be she, I trow."

"'Tis witchery, fer certain sure," muttered the widow, hastily stuffing the coney net into the folds of her apron. "How cometh it that thou be'st here?"

"Ah, word gets 'round," replied the old woman vaguely. "Tut. Let us not bandy words, for ye came to fetch me and here be I." Up rose she and twitched her inky garments closer about her.

In wonder, the village men and village layabouts gawped as the procession of eight women trooped back into the village, the stooped, obscure figure of the forest crone trudging meekly amidst seven stern faces. Up lept Magistrate Mickle, choking on his pot of ale as the village women marched the witch straight up to his bower bench on the commons.

"Now, do thy duty, Mickle, and condemn her, seein' as how we've fetched 'er 'ere," demanded those seven vengeful sisters.

"Aye," said the Magistrate, mopping ale from his stippled beard. "That I will and anon. But yet, the Law requires that we establish plain she be a practitioner of Darkness and Heresy."

"Hast thou not been listening, Blunderhead?" howled the villagers as one. "Over this path have we tromped already! If the Law requires more, why, the Law must be a fool and an ass."

"Still and all," insisted the Magistrate loftily, "its Will must be respected right and proper. How shalt we deliver proof 'gainst this evil person?"

"Why, let us burn her at the stake," said Dame

Marjorie. "If the wood will not light, 'tis a sure sign of her witchery."

"Nay, nay! Let us dangle her from a gibbet, feet o'er head; and if the ravens pluck not out her eyes within a fortnight, then we will know for certain a witch she be," reasoned Twisty Earl.

"Too slow, too slow," blurted Goodwife Beatrix. "Let us fling her down yonder well! Should she float therein, why, 'tis all the proof we need of her witchcraft. Then we can haul her out and stone her forthwith."

"Hmm," pondered Magistrate Mickle, "Sage counsel all this be. Whilst I think on't, let us conduct one small formality. Madam Witch, what hath thou to offer in thine own defense? And, prithee, make it brief, for the sun grows warm and I feel a grave thirst comin' on."

The old woman peered slowly 'round from 'neath her grey and beetled brow into the faces of all her neighbors, one by one.

"Dim doth the light of mercy shine amongst ye, I see," she said, her survey done. "Well, 'tis true. I have used the craft and knowledge I ha' gleaned from close study and careful observation, lo, these many years. And, few of ye there be that have not come to me in secret at midnight for counsel or relief. The which, by-the-by, have I lent most gladly.

"Much good it has done me or ye," continued this beldame in a low voice. "For, human nature lies beyond my ken to transform. In the end, we are that which we are, for better or ill."

"Blameth thou us for thy perfidy then?" interrupted Magistrate Mickle.

"'Tis not the stars that do make us what we are,"

replied the old one. "Seek out Evil and we find it at home. Look for the Good, and that, too, appeareth anon. Ye citizens, good and true, ha' decided I must be what thou perceiveth me to be, e'en though ye but peer into a mirror of glass at thine own selves."

"'Tis the Devil's own sophistry," shouted Goodwife Gretchen at the crone's words.

"Aye! Best we stone the witch here 'n now, afore she pours more poison into our ears," asserted Brother Dwindle.

"Convinced am I," said Magistrate Mickle, nervously looking o'er the heated crowd. "The Law be well satisfied, I ween."

Just then, a deep, loud voice boomed: "Well then—thou and the Law must be disappointed in this instance." Out from the seething crowd stepped a powerful figure wrapped from head to knee in a cloak of forest green. Beneath this cloak protruded the silken cuffs of scarlet pantaloons, and from this bearded stranger's ear, there gleamed a ring of silver.

"Speak of the Devil," gasped Dame Dulthea, whilst Brother Dwindle dropped to his knees and groped for his wooden beads.

"Speak of whome'er ye wish," thundered the stranger. "I care not, for I have need of this eld woman."

Fast into the generous folds of his forest green cape he quickly wrapped the hag. In a flash and a cloud of azure smoke, the twain had vanished, leaving all the villagers bleary eyed and coughing.

Past sunset and long after moonrise, in a mean cottage hidden deep within the forest, sat the crone and the potent djinn o'er a pot of root tea and platter of oat cakes, while the old woman's dog and cat dozed before a humble fire burning low.

"Thou certainly took thy sweet time in appearing. I was sore afeared that I might needs metamorph into a bird or beast and thus escape," complained she.

"Truly sorry about that I am," replied the djinn meekly. "'Twas more difficult than I expected to choose the proper cloak in color, size and weave. And, well thou knowst that, for those of us in our craft, the show be nigh all that counts—show and a bold manner and a puff of smoke and thunder. But come; are we not safe enow now?"

"For the nonce," replied his dear old wife. "Yet, I feel that the Age of Miracles waneth fast whilst the Age of Skepticism and Fear cometh on apace—which bodes ill for the likes o' us. As thou hath seen, folk of late have need of scapegoats more than e'er before; and who better than them that already be the black sheep of the flock? So be it. Times do change and so must we.

"And, as we be speaking of change, in what form wouldst thou have me tonight?" the crone continued. "A sweetly scented bride from the odah? A milkmaid with golden braids? Mayhap a lusty tavern wench? That be my favorite, I confess, and so hath it been e'er since that night in Tripoli."

Broadly beamed the splendid djinn upon her. "Be but thyself, as thou truly art, and my heart shall dance the faster."

"E'en with stooped back, wizened face, wiry hair and rheumy eye?"

"Nothing better," said the magnificent djinn, folding his powerful arms across his broad chest. "Is not old wine tastier and the more satisfying?"

"Oh Dennis, thou wert ever a smooth one, thou sly dog," grinned she then. "Come here now and douse the candle."

Tale the Thirtieth
The Crone Bids Farewell...For Now

In a mean dwelling deep within a dark forest, where the lane ends and no one now dares go, the old crone sat alone beside her hearth fire, wherein a few dying embers yet glowed. Well past moonrise 'twas—had there been a moon to rise—and dark as pitch was the starry vault above. Yet, in the deep eyes of the eld one gleamed the light of days and deeds long past.

In silent communion, her loyal familiars drowsed—the black cat napping on her lap and the tawny dog a-snoring at her feet. At last, the old woman bestirred herself to announce aloud:

"Most loyal and truest friends, I ween the time has come—as such moments must do—to bid thee *adieu* and also forsake the villages and hamlets and towns, woods, fields and fells here 'round. For, there is naught to keep me a-lingering any longer."

At this pronouncement, the cat stretched leisurely upon the beldame's apron, offering this cool observation the while (ye will recall that the crone had gifted both animals the power of speech to make the long night the less tedious):

"Mistress, surely I be not hearing thee aright. Why would anyone leave such a fine place as this? 'Tis warm and dry and cometh with ample supply of cream and mice."

Up roused the dog as well, and he gazed piteously into the woman's wizened face. "Aye, Good Madam, for once yon cat sayeth something true! We be warm and safe here, where neither stranger nor foe dares trouble us...save a runaway child or two now and again," concluded the dog lamely.

"More like am I to drain the ocean, dear friends, or to wipe the stars clean from the welkin, than to justify the whys and wherefores of this old heart. All I know is that Life calls me hence, and I must go to meet my Fate, whate'er and where'er it be. Yet, though I leave this place and time, I shall remember it in tales and songs of our adventurous deeds."

"But, dear Mistress, hast thou considered fully how thou shalt live and what thou shalt eat?" queried the cat, suspicion narrowing her golden eyes.

"I have—and 'twill be no problem. For many years those hapless brigands, Lesley and Dinkin, have plied their shifty trade to my benefit; and now I have gold and silver and jewels enow to live like Queen Sheba, durst I wish to."

"Yet, wither shalt thou go?" asked the dog, his alarm growing apace.

"That I canna say for certain. I hear tell that the New World shall offer places to slake the thirst of one so interested in change as I. There's the 'land of flowers' ruled by the Spanish king, and the English will soon ha' their Jamestown, I believe. I might next journey north to New Amsterdam—and, following that, there'll be a village called Salem, all which I am most curious to see."

"Recall ye not what curiosity did to the cat?" observed the dour cat.

"Those be strange sounding places and far away," the dog whined. "And, pray tell, what shalt we two poor beasts do there?"

"Alas, good friends, ye may not company me, I fear. Light of foot, hand and heart must I be for now, knowing not what might befall. Nor know I where I shalt go first or where I'll dwell at last."

"Again, good Mistress, what, in the meantime, becomes of us?" persisted the dog.

"Why, I shouldna worry. Ye be clever animals, and this Old World will always welcome talking beasts, doubt it not. 'Twould be a small wonder were ye not to make thy fortunes from thy wits and glib tongues."

"True, we *are* wonders, to be sure," agreed the cat. "And I, at least, am most loveable, when all is said and done. Yet, entertaining burghers with words and antics and jibes seems a chancy venture; and I be far from certain this dog here shall be much good at it."

"What! Can I not roll over and beg for my supper as well as the next 'un?" protested the indignant dog.

"Well-a-day; let that vile canard lie," he plowed on. "What shall become of the magic when you've gone? How shalt these baffled people fare?"

"Ah, 'twas never true magic," said the old woman; "leastways not like in the **Dark Ages** of yore. 'Twas more like holding up a finger to see which way the wind did blow and then sailing before it as doth a kite. I suppose the people will go on about their ordinary business in their ordinary ways, speaking their ordinary language and leading their ordinary lives...lives in which, without my help, no one transforms to stone nor dances with a moon nor vanishes into the forest nor gazes at a star . . ."

"What be a *kite*, dear Mistress?" asked the dog, interrupting her lofty flight of rhetoric.

"Merely a thing of string and paper that needeth only wind and imagination to soar," replied the old woman, her faraway look lingering.

"But to whom shalt them good people turn in times of need?" craftily pressed the cat. "Dost not thou owe them further sage counsel and advice?"

"The World we know is changing apace, I fear," she replied. "Seldom do folk summon me at midnight anymore; nor do they welcome some dark figure making cryptic comments and veiled warnings at cradle- or grave-side. They're oft more like to think they're Masters of their Fates that dwell where Good and Evil are as plain to see as Day and Night—never ye mind the many hours they puzzle o'er Right and Wrong in the gloaming or through all the night's watches."

"Perhaps we could persuade 'em to rise up later or take to their pallets a tad earlier," offered the dog hopefully.

"How wide thou doth always miss the point!" hissed the cat. And, turning to the crone, she pressed her argument forward: "But, Mistress, dost thou not fear that thy work be unfinished or may come undone? I perceive there's still a plenteous store of Stupidity and Cruelty and Selfishness and simple Foul Nature to go 'round."

"A point well-taken, my dear feline! Yet, do thou remember: my powers can do little to alter people's natures. Their hearts—in the main—be good; but their wits and wills be as chaff swirling about in winter's winds— especially when the matter touches hard upon their self-regard. Then, they take the World as swaddling for them alone, there to warm them and provide them with victuals and wealth and love and victories small and great, no matter how ill others fare.

"I fear that goodly change, if 'tis to come at all, must come to each heart itself—and that transformation be most difficult and slow."

"Thou hast a very low opinion of mankind, I see," observed the dog. "Were then all our clever gins and enchanted adventures naught but failures?"

"Do not despair, my friend. We've worked many small wonders and altered some situations—and, though small wonders they were, they were still *wondrous* strange! Now, I'll see what 'magic' I can do in pastures and woodlands new and leave the betterment o' mankind here to others. For now, I must bid ye *Farewell.*"

"Yet stay, dear mistress, but a moment more," moaned the dog. "When shall we three meet again?"

"That I canna foretell," apologized the crone. "Yet, meet again we shalt, I ha' no doubt. This Mighty Globe is round as a ripe pippin (though few do credit that as yet), and 'tis a small Globe after all.

"Nor is Time anything but a child's toy that we may spin and twirl as we will—if not in fact, then certainly in tales and songs and grand gests. True friends always shall meet again to tell of their brave trials and adventures. 'Til that good day dawns, I say, *Farewell, my dears, farewell!*"

At this, that old woman sprang up with the agility of one half her age. In the wink o' a lamb's eye, she'd snatched up her twisty staff, her bag and her sheaf of scribbled pages, twitched her ancient mantle about her tight, and vanished into the pitchy night.

At this, the dog let out a long and piteous howl, the likes of which would rouse dead souls.

"Thou wert always so sentimental a poor creature," sighed the cat, this time with unalloyed kindness. "Do hush now. For, we have winding lanes and paths and leagues to go before we sleep."

Apologia

Dennis and the cat think 'tis a great waste o' time to send this little book out into such a strange New World as this...and it may be they are right.

Why should anyone these days take an interest in the musty tales of an ancient crone—some that arise from my travels and travails, some that spring like dreams from mine own imaginings? After all, there be brash rumors and incredible theories aplenty flying around us now, and no one today knows (or seems to care) from whom or whence those falsehoods come.

Nor ha' I yet mastered this brave, new tongue that buzzeth through the very ether like wasps aswarm about my poor head. *Strange and new*, 'tis what I sought—and that is what I've found.

Still, new as this World is, I see herein a glimmering, like a lone candle in the darkest night, of the World I once knew, the olden world I mused upon and built castles in the air upon many a long, lonely watch beside a dying fire.

There is a ray of discovery there that I hope shall guide thy days, gentle readers.

How long I linger here, I know not. It may be that my arts—limited as they be—will avail me naught, and I must move on perforce. It may be that I find the means to bring about whate'er good I can do here, if in a new guise and under a different name. As ever, Time and Circumstance will tell the tale.

Know ye, also, that there be more gests and stories where these came from. 'Tis our natures to seek relief, laughter, fright and answers to the confused and noisy world around us in fables, tales and songs.

And so, I keep a-scribbling; for, it gladdens my heart and eases my fears. Tonight, shall I venture forth again, seeking one of weak will and sagging spirits who may help launch my little book into this strange, new place and time.

But now, as I take my leave, the dog hath urged me to pen this wee verse:

> *Now ye've heard these tales of mine,*
> *At once both old and new,*
> *Of tumult, chance, of tears and change;*
> *The rest—'tis down to you.*

Acknowledgements

With apologies to John Donne, no book is an island—and none comes into being without the contributions of many. I'd like to thank a few of them here.

First, I owe a huge debt to those who founded and explored the folk and fairytale genre: from Ovid and Aesop to "Mother Goose," the Brothers Grimm, Hans Christian Andersen, and the many Irish and Appalachian balladeers and on to more recent storytellers like James Branch Cabell (*Jurgen*), Anne Sexton (*Transformations*), Goldman and Reiner (*The Princess Bride*—screenplay and film) and even the Disney studios sanitized tales and the screwball "Fractured Fairy Tales" of the old *Rocky and Bullwinkle* show. They've fed my imagination and opened up possibilities in both direct and subliminal ways. Where my efforts fall short of the bar they've raised, the fault is mine alone.

Closer to home, several close friends have given me valued feedback at earlier stages of this project, and I want to thank them—in particular, Laura and Dennis for their encouragement, and Steve, my "good physician" friend, for his cheerful assurances. Warmest thanks are also due to Victoria and Calvin, whose suggestions in our writing workshops opened my eyes to fresh possibilities. Finally, I wish to acknowledge the enduring memory of Georg Gaston, who insisted that every writer must first believe in him- or herself.

To Nick and the crew at Atmosphere Press: thank you for seeing an opportunity where others did not. Every new author should be lucky enough to find so adventurous a publisher.

Above all, I've had the remarkably good fortune to have found a "true friend and a good writer" in my life's partner. Her good taste, humor and warmth make everything possible, and I am grateful, Elizabeth, beyond words.

About Atmosphere Press

Atmosphere Press is an independent, full-service publisher for excellent books in all genres and for all audiences. Learn more about what we do at atmospherepress.com.

We encourage you to check out some of Atmosphere's latest releases, which are available at Amazon.com and via order from your local bookstore:

Newer Testaments, a novel by Philip Brunetti
All Things in Time, a novel by Sue Buyer
Hobson's Mischief, a novel by Caitlin Decatur
The Black-Marketer's Daughter, a novel by Suman Mallick
The Farthing Quest, a novel by Casey Bruce
This Side of Babylon, a novel by James Stoia
Within the Gray, a novel by Jenna Ashlyn
For a Better Life, a novel by Julia Reid Galosy
Where No Man Pursueth, a novel by Micheal E. Jimerson
Here's Waldo, a novel by Nick Olson
Tales of Little Egypt, a historical novel by James Gilbert
The Hidden Life, a novel by Robert Castle
Big Beasts, a novel by Patrick Scott
Alvarado, a novel by John W. Horton III
Nothing to Get Nostalgic About, a novel by Eddie Brophy
GROW: A Jack and Lake Creek Book, a novel by Chris S McGee
Home is Not This Body, a novel by Karahn Washington
Whose Mary Kate, a novel by Jane Leclere Doyle
Stuck and Drunk in Shadyside, a novel by M. Byerly

About the Author

J. D. Jahn is a retired communicator who lives in St. Augustine, Florida. *The Crone's Tales* marks his debut as a published writer of fiction. He earned a Ph.D. in British Renaissance literature and taught college-level English and writing before joining a series of college and university foundations as a writer/editor/communications manager. He has authored several scholarly articles and poems as well as numerous magazine articles, newsletters, annual reports, solicitations and other promotional materials. Currently, he's completing a follow-up suite of crone's tales and, with his wife, writing a crime novel set in Brooklyn, NY.

CPSIA information can be obtained
at www.ICGtesting.com
Printed in the USA
LVHW020803221221
706863LV00004B/485